"82"

Year of the Monster

Brandon Burnside

Copyright 2020 by Brandon Burnside

All Rights Reserved.

No part of this book may be reproduced in any manner without written permission except in the case of brief quotations embodied in articles and reviews.

Although the author has made every effort to ensure that the information in this book was correct at press time, the author does not assume and hereby disclaim any liability to any party for any loss, damage, or disruption caused by errors or omissions, whether such errors or omissions result from negligence, accident, or any other cause. Forms and agreements are included for informational purpose only.

Editor: Paul LeBlond

Formatted and published by: Adil Sultan

You can find Adil Sultan here, visit:
https://www.fiverr.com/adilsultan1

Table of Contents

Chapter 1 The mirror tells all 1
Chapter 2 The long ride 9
Chapter 3 Maddison Stranz 13
Chapter 4 Another kill 20
Chapter 5 The Body Shop gym 25
Chapter 6 Father knows best 31
Chapter 7 The blood bath sign 35
Chapter 8 A killer's work is never done 42
Chapter 9 Maddison's nightmares 48
Chapter 10 Victor Cruz 50
Chapter 11 The Takeover 56
Chapter 12 I see you 58
Chapter 13 I am home, Baby 64
Chapter 14 The escape 67
Chapter 15 On my way home 69
Chapter 16 The FBI 72
Chapter 17 My waking 75
Chapter 18 Love spell 82
Chapter 19 Hard times 86
Chapter 20 The killing machines 91
Chapter 21 Florida State Prison 96

Chapter 1
The mirror tells all

My name is Brody Bransford. I stood there naked contemplating on what would look good on me for the night. My looks were very boss as I worked out to pump my muscles to their full bellies to gorge to the fulfillment of my shape. Had to be perfect was my motto. The old bastard told me over and over when I was young enough not to know an asshole when I saw one. The blood shed I wished for my pops. "The old degenerate prick!" I shouted." Wham," my hand destroyed the glass shattering it to the sink in big and small pieces. My hand was vibrating uncontrollably to the utter point of annoyance from the sheer pain of the cut. I checked my hand, "You fucked your hand up buddy boy!" I muttered to myself. The hand had to get stitches now or probably fuck it. It was 1982 and boy what a year it had been already. My anger was raging at the thought of the prick, Tony Bransford, my father and the monster wanted him dead I felt also, even though he was after women.

I had been a very handsome man to the point of greatness I felt, my cleft chin a staple of brawn. I had the greenest eyes that had made the ladies swoon over me when I worked out at the gym during the day. I had that kind of hair that looked as if I were a twin for Billy idol. I wore a cross in my left ear to show I was a pretty cool dude. At a young age of 25, I brushed my hair to a tease giving it that rocker vibe. I was a man's man and nobody would ever doubt me otherwise. "You are a fine ass man!" I spoke. Fuck, I knew I had to get to the gym or my boss would eat my ass up for the third tardy this week.

The body shop gym had been my heaven and also my hell, I had a crush on a Maddison Stranz. She had thought I was creepy, which I was. I thought about my next pump and the thrill it gave me.

When I went to the local bar I would get free drinks from the hot-as-hell bartender, Ginger. She always gave free shots to the beefy Brody Bransford, the body builder.

My mind came back from the last daydream. I had been feeling some side effects of the 'roids, or steroids, as was the technical name. "Test", or testosterone, had been the key in gaining my size. But my balls had taken a hit, and I mean a major hit, as if they had shrunk to little raisins. My junk also did not work most of the time and chicks had it coming as the spirit of the killer inside loved women. Killing them and taking out their eyes had been the monster's m.o. and now I had it inside me and it was uncontrollable.

My needle was sitting on top of his septic tank. It had a full dosage of test. I licked my lips as a tasty new treat would be in real quick. I hated it when the needle went in and it hurt like hell when it burned after. I sat on the toilet ready for the injection, my veins were vascular as hell and the road map was an easy place to find one or many of the little suckers. The yellow liquid was pure I thought as I had scored it off one of men in the locker room. I got it as a great deal, a "brother's deal" as Jimmy Bell had said.

The syringe pushed the liquid into the blood stream allowing for the testosterone to take its course and giving me more power now:

"I love this shit and I am not going to stop for shit!" I scolded myself. I was going to be bigger than Arnold if it killed me in the process. I sat there for another few minutes and flexed for the crowed as I was a contender in the Mr. Olympia contest, my pearly whites were bright, they loved my smile I thought. I was ready for the day and I had the juice. My eyes felt weak as the monster took over my body, my vision was blurry when the monster took over me.

I hated my father with a passion. When I was 18 years old, I had a chance, after Tony beat the hell out of me, as I had come home late one night. The gun was there and I should have killed him when I had the chance. Tony had a major fall last year as he was working on the house, his foot had slipped and he fell a good few stories breaking his back in different places. He has not been able to walk to this day. The good son had been there to take care of him everyday for the last 4 months. "I need my pills!" my father shouted at me from the bedroom in the two story house. My mom had passed away one night as she had hit her head in the kitchen. I had suspected my dad of doing it with pleasure. It was funny as he had a new girlfriend shortly after. "Where's my pills, boy! Hey, I am talking to you!" His voice was evil as evil was. My father had been a horrid father in my life. What a drunk he was. "Hope you choke on your pills." As I turned my head in fright from the scolding and all the beatings I had taken as boy and a man. Life was tough but somehow I managed to get through the day. "You hope what?" My old man called out to me. Nothing pops. I was done with the mirror as I now had to fix it before my dad would see it sometime in the future. I would get whipped within an inch of my life for something like that.

    I crossed to my father's room with a readiness to please the old man. Knock knock, "Come in shit head!" Tony said with aggravation in his voice. Tony laid there in the home hospital bed. It was motorized and could easily go up and down by the remote control. Nothing but the best for the old bastard I thought to myself. My father's eyes swollen from lack of sleep, the brown eyes that tortured my soul for years of pain, I felt when seeing this man's eyes. Tony had the look of an asshole, his hair short as a crew cut from serving in the military for 10 years. He liked it that way and despised long hair that was unruly and unkempt he had thought. What kind of man wore his hair to his shoulders but queers, he scolded random people sometimes about their hair. His face shaven to the point of not having one long hair.

    I was In charge of getting him his razors from the local shop. His once muscled look turned to fat from the binges of drinking hard liquor throughout the day. I wondered why he had not died of liver disease sooner or would that ever happen.

    I had been coy and playing his game of cat and mouse as I was not in charge of my life but just a pawn of some sort, moving piece by piece as my strategy was to kill him one day with a butcher knife or just strangle him to death. Maybe beat him by the hammer as the monster liked to kill his victims. Morbid thoughts ran through my mind as if you were to think about what you wanted to eat for the day. It made me happy the thought of killing in general. I had seen Halloween in 1978 at the drive-in with Martha, my old broad that I used to fuck quite often and for kicks I would cum in her without a condom. She really did turn me on when I still think about it. The part where Michael kills his sister really gave me a hard on and I loved fucking her during the killing scene. That was before I was full of muscles and I was a fat boy, as the kids called me. Her glasses where rad and I loved how she would fix them when she rode me. I liked having the Firebird then and it was a pussy wetter. "Brody, can I ask you a question?" I could remember her eyes clear as night with a little bit cross-eyedness to them. I dreamt of taking her life and then fucking her brain's out. Was I sick or did most people think this way? My thoughts were always running wild.

"What's the question, Martha?" I asked her in anticipation of the hilarious question she would ask. The windows were fogged up from the passionate sex we had that night. She had kept her top on as not cause a reaction from the on lookers that strolled by the red Firebird. "Why do you like me?" She had asked a funny question and how the hell do I know. My laughter came out as I spat up some of my coke-a-cola I had been drinking. The burning taste gave me acid reflux. Her eyes were squinting and she was about to cry hysterically in my face and I could not accept that type of action.

Pussies cried, my good old daddy would say. "I am sorry Martha, I was just thinking about something funny I saw on TV." I had been chill as ice, I was in charge of her. She could not resist me in anyway. "You are...you know..." My words just died at that moment and I had nothing I could say to her to give her answers she desired. My eyes turned away as she kept staring at me with her baby blues.

I was immature at the time and broke up with good old Martha.

I had killed one chick before and she was a hooker named Kim Fiora that I picked up in my white Ford van and hit her head with a hammer and scooped her eyes out like ice cream. My emotions sometimes got a hold of me as the monster wants to come out to play.

"What are you doing dumbass?" I was lost as my mind had slipped away from reality to the past 4 years with Martha. Whack! The sound was loud as the motherfucker hit me. I fell back crashing into the chair that was behind me. The old rocking chair that had been my mother's before she had passed. I hit my head with such force, I blacked out as if it had been a dream. "You were dreaming." Tony said to me as if I had been in another world. It was weird how I could be day dreaming and have a lump on my head afterwords. The bastard hit me. Why do I let him hurt me, I could break every bone in his body like that.

1982 had been a shit year and things were going to change like it or not. "Give me my pills boy or I am going to knock your teeth out!" His hand had been raised as I had been a dog or some cornered animal. He will learn and it will come when he least expects it. "What pills are you shouting about pops?" He must have been talking about his candy, he loved to pop the pills daily with the hard liquor. It had been his medicine as he had a tin flask next to his bed. Maybe if I put some drain cleaner in it for you next time. All I could do was smile and tell myself that he still had another 30 years or so to go. He must have meant pain pills as I looked for his pills. The orange bottle was laying on the floor next to his bed. The bottle was empty like he had taken all 90 capsules of the super strong pills. "Pops you had taken them all." I knew he was an addict of the powdery form kind as well.

Tony's bat coming for the home run knocks the bottle, flying across the room.

His breath was ill, smelled of old garbage and liquor. Tony tried to get me, but his back just collapsed. His face in agony as the injuries had not healed all the way. Every time I get near him something happens. He is not a good person, but he did give you life I had thought with pain in my mind. My hands wrapped around his throat, that would shut him up, I cracked a small smile.

The clock chimed 8:30am as I was scheduled for my first client Miss Buxton, Sharon Buxton, now that was a women to fight for, her wealth was over the 10 million mark as I was guessing. Her brand new Mercedes was a beauty with the custom leather seats that you pay extra for at the snobby place called the Mercedes dealer in Tampa. Her yellow beauty as she called it to me.

I remember her always asking me if I wanted a ride and she knew I loved being spoiled. One night after our training session, I would take her car for a spin to Dave's Rock On Club, where the Who's Who in the Tampa Bay Area went for their needs to be met with coke and their alcohol fixes. As I looked back at my father, his eyes closed as he had passed out from his drunken stupor. He laid there like the dead. Snoring like the fat pig that he was. The tin flask sat there in front of me. The initials had been carved and read for the Great Tony Bransford, his mark would be a total bitch as I see it. He bitches all day and drives me crazy.

The outside weather was a bright and sunny day as it always was in the greater Tampa Bay area. Carrollwood was a nice place where nothing really bad ever happened. The neighbors knew your names or at least said, 'hi', with a smile in tow. I liked to look good as I wore my polo shirt tight and fitted, the color was best when it had dark colors to hide my imperfections. The tight shirts fit me quite well with the dumbbell logo that hung snugly on my nipple. Earrings were not allowed due to having a professional look. As soon as I was out I punked it like Billy Idol would.

The Firebird was sleek and streamlined for a '78', not bad for a boy from a middle class neighborhood. The paint sparkled as if every one of them shined to perfection. The turtle wax always did such a great job.

The paper was out and the head story had read, "Woman brutally killed and eyes were scooped out and not found". Ahh, my work had been found and I wondered how long it would take? The young chick had been easy prey for me. She had been at the bar that night alone and she had been a prostitute and sadden by her breakup from her ex and she had planned on going out and getting laid that night. She did not expect to end up dead from a night of fun. Her eyes were fun to carve out so she could not tell with her eyes as I remember it all. The night had been a week ago in early February. The spot had been a dive bar that I had not been to before and was an hour away from me. I did not want to get caught as I had no need for prison, my insides burned hard as the urge caught up with me and I had to act on it. The bar's name had been The Dead Pool, what a name for it, right?

The town was Clearwater and it was a pretty quiet night. When I walked into that scene, the counters were wooded as if the wood had been shined and dipped in something varnished. The lights were dim as it was best not to be noticed. The female sat there as if her world was lost. Her blonde hair did it for that night although I was hoping for a red head, that would have been the ticket. Martha was quite the red head and that's what turned me on. The mohawked bartender stood focused on me as if I looked like someone she had known. I had looked like a rocker, I had been her type I guess. My hair was not teased as I wore a pair of shades to cover my green eyes that were a dead ringer for me. My chin had a full beard now to hide away my trade mark well-defined cleft chin. I could still pull this woman at any cost. Good thing I had a van and it was not the flashy Firebird that would for sure get me busted quicker than shit. Her smell was sweet like apples when a twinge of it hit my nose, the smell for sure was going to stick with me like cancer. Her red lipstick got me weak at the knees because it reminded me of blood and that was a turn on. Her big busty chest stood erect as a sailor saluting his officer. Her dress had been a simple blue polka-dotted dress as if she had been doing the retro thing. I sat down next to her but a little bit of fear hit me as talking to them always made me nervous. "What are you drinking?" "I am drinking a Vodka tonic, a lady has to keep her figure...you know?" She was gorgeous as she had my attention unlike the rest of the people who were invisible to me. I snapped my fingers as the bartender hurried over as if she was doing her job to perfection. "Get her another...Vodka tonic." My smile was wide as if I couldn't keep shut my mouth. My teeth were white and a smile goes a long way I thought. "You want to go back to my place, stud?" Her hand proceeded to my thigh as she knew how to get my attention for sure. My cock was hard and her hand massaged it. Her taste was delicious, she kissed me and turned me on. But we needed to get her to her place fast.

I paid with cash and didn't leave my name with anyone. "You look like Billy...Idol," she said to me. I shied away as I was paying the tip, did not want to get remembered as being the Billy Idol look alike. I gave a slight laugh as she had no idea why. I took her hand and I did not even know her name. Well, we don't have to say anything about that I thought as she would be another dead one with no eyes. As the monster grew more evil.

Chapter 2
The long ride

I felt a sharp pain in stomach as a copper passed me doing at least 75 miles per hour in a 45, he must have been chasing someone or something, I could say.

The night had been perfect as I took her in my van and I did not even have to drug her this time. I always felt like I had too, but when you are a stud like me, even Billy Idol could not have got her quicker in his van if he drove one.

The sign read St. Pete, I was at least 40 mins away from Tampa as I liked to be when I unleashed the monster as I called it. I did not know the monster until this year, 1982, and I had not believed I would have killed my first one. The feeling was like Christmas, as you know everyone waits for Santa to come bring them presents, we always laid out the big delicious chocolate chip cookies as mom had made them fresh. I always loved when she made them for me.

The van had been blacked-out for the windows as when I drove to get my victims, they would not have been seen. It was against the law to have blacked-out windows as you might have kidnapped a girl or a boy if you liked that kind of thing.

The van always had a hammer under the seat if I had to kill my prey or at least knock them out so they would not fight back. The old van ran good, I had bought it for cash from one of the people from the newspaper. I had only paid $500 dollars for such a nice van. The van had some rust spots as it was not new. It was a 1970's Ford and was quite good and they lasted forever. The gas had been filled as the journey was long sometimes trying to find the right one, stopping quite often might have cost me my life later on.

As I looked at her and all I can think of is taking her back and fucking her brains out and then taking her eyes out so the cops can't see who did it, I might be a little crazy but if you know the saying...see no evil, hear no evil. The paper had been guessing at who might have killed the girl, no one would ever find out. I washed the body with alcohol and that would kill my DNA or anything tied to me. "Where do you live?" "To be honest...I don't go home with strangers but I could not resist your sexy look. You're so handsome!" Her expression was excited I could tell and I loved being told how good I look. "Thanks babe, and you look damn hot too, I love your lipstick!" She smiled with her full lips, she had the sexiest top lip I had ever seen. "What do they call you?" I loved her style as I did enjoy the 50's look and the polka dots really fit her. She made turned me on. Snap out of it, you are not trying to wife this one, stupid. I was slipping and I had to keep my cool or I might fall for this one. "Angie, that's what my friends call me, love, but you can call me your girlfriend," as she told me, I saw her cheeks were getting red. "Yeah maybe you could be girlfriend material and better yet wife material." She looked away smiling like a kid that got their candy from the Easter bunny.

She sat there staring into my eyes like a love-sick love bird. "Are we going to go back to your house, Angie?" I was curious if I could come over and spend sometime with her before you know what I mean. She sat there cooly lighting up a smoke and I knew this type of girl loved to smoke. Her long nails had a rather yellow nicotine from all the years she had smoked. Her fingers lifted the cig as it was so correct and so lovely, it made it hard to kill this one I swear on it. The drive had been going on for what seemed like hours. As I checked my Casio watch, it read 12am on the dot. It was not the witching hour but more or less a kind of pre- witching hour. The last time I killed had been at 2am when we had sex. The part of sex always got me excited, the steroids made it sometimes hard to get that rock hard erection as the veins in my body were there as if a road map was made from my veins showcasing the towns of the surrounding Florida. "We are going to the beach and I've got a surprise for you." Her blue eyes were like the oceans waves crashing down on me hard. Her eyes fluttered as she spoke.

My stomach had butterflies flying around as the monster was going away for the night. The monster would come back tomorrow or the next day and I could not stop it. If I start to care for her I might be fucking myself, I was a man and I sure as hell had feelings for the opposite sex. I was not a queer for sure because I had been invited in the steam room with several of my clients. They wanted to blow me, but I told them I would pass because well, they did not turn me on like a woman with big honkers.

The sea had been rather beautiful tonight as the stars were out shining bright. I could see many different ones as I tried to find the brightest star like Pinocchio had said. The waves crashed the sea wall spilling some of water on us, it was cold for this time of year as it was still winter, but in Florida was always like summer time. I saw they had fixed the old dock, it had several holes in it from being very old and city not putting money on it to fix it.

What do you do for a living "Billy Idol"? Oh shit, and what should I tell her, she was so into me and I couldn't get out of it if I wanted to now. I work at a gym in Tampa, I teach the members how to get their pump on. I flexed my muscles as they were huge, her boobs might have been just as humongous as my arms were. Her eyes were fixed on me like a rocket locking on to a target flying around. "I am kinda good at what I do." Angie got up, showed me her body with her bra on now, but she whipped it off with a flash of the hand and her nipples were rock hard, they were cute and not too big. They reminded me of perky nipples which were always my choice over the big saucers that all big titties had. "I told you I had a secret." Her face was playful as her wrinkles started to show as she smiled more and made me feel like passing out from not following my plan. Her bra flew off with thunderous finger session flinging the bra above her head like a rodeo cowgirl catching her bull with the rope. Her nipples were pink as not quite ripe strawberries, but who did not like strawberries. I moved closer to her as I could, her eyes locked onto me as I was on to hers. Our lips slowly came in for a romantic kiss. I could taste the rep lipstick as it was bitter from the makeup and it must have been untasteable lip gloss, I know she set out for a man tonight to make love, I kinda knew that as she grabbed my cock in that bar. She pulled away as I was trying to get more of her lips, she made me horny and I did want her badly. "I am going on for a swim," she pushed away from me like she had played coy to get me interested in her. Martha had been nothing like this sexy blond woman, her face, her killer curves were out of this world and I knew I could not take her life. We had something now and it was blossoming as I had treated her like a real person. That was the mistake I had made. The monster was fighting and I felt burning through my body when he wanted to consume his victims. But no, Angie was not the same as the Clearwater hooker. She had made me pay for it and that did not sit well with me, who the hell pays when you are just so perfect like I am. My plan had failed as I had come this far and had not made a kill and I fell for her, she would be my downfall and put me in prison if she ever found out. She never would because I would kill Angie for sure. The night flew by as I followed her, naked as jaybird in the sea as my new girlfriend. I most likely would not make it in for my appointment with a client later on today, fuck it, I found something that turned me on for once without having to kill to get turned on. I laughed to myself as I was changing a little for now, the monster would strike another one soon.

Chapter 3
Maddison Stranz

Maddison Stranz stood there, skimming over the daily goals as a new detective within the Tampa police department. She had been working the field for the last two years, as a new recruit, she had placed in the top 5 out a class of more than 50 recruits. It had always been a goal for Maddison to be the spitting image of her old man James Stranz. Her father had been killed when she was only 12 years old and leaving her at such a young age. She strived to be her very best as did her father. "These scum need to be apprehended soon. One case had been bothering me and I need to get to the bottom of it." Maddison had the looks of a beauty queen and she did not take shit whatsoever. Her short, blond hair had made her look almost butch, but when she was out of her suit she had been a blockbuster of a woman. Her slender five-foot five inch tall frame, made her more of a smaller woman. Her radiant blue eyes were a knock out. Her boobs had looked dynamite in a sports bra when she attended the Body Shop gym. One guy at the gym kept hitting on her and she turned him down every time, but she had not been able to lose this guy that looked like Billy Idol. He had been super muscular and sexy to boot, but he had given her creepy vibes. He seemed to be almost like a stalker. Good thing she always carried her 38-Special and it was not the police issued one that all the cops had gotten. This was from her dad as she had kept it all these years. Maddison had been preparing herself since she was in diapers.

A few weeks earlier she had visited the house where the young woman had been mutilated and the eyes taken. Well, let's say that they were missing and only sockets had sat there like red rabbit holes. The killer had left one thing that might lead Maddison in the capture of the monster who did it. She had traces of semen in her vaginal canal. There had been blood from tearing the vaginal canal. Maddison's face was a wreck from the thought of this person that could fuck the girl and then take out her eyes. Her head had been busted to the temples with some blunt force trauma. The hole of about one inch around. It seemed have been a pin hammer of some sort. Whack! Maddison swung her arm as she was pretending to be the killer and to use the pressure from the swing. As she dropped her hand as the captain walked in. "Miss Stranz, I see you are practicing your tennis lessons for today?"

Dennis McDonald has had a rather "no playing around" mentality as his motto for the 22nd Precinct as captain of this place for the past 30 years. Maddison had been hoping to have him retire by this time next year for 1983. Maybe one day she could run the show as she had thought for the past two years. "Miss Stranz!" Denis shouted to wake her out of her day dream. What can I expect from my all-star and I do mean you Miss Stranz? Do you have any leads so far?" Denis was an overweight man in his 60's that smoked way too much as he smelled like an ashtray. His combover style hair cut had been very good on him but his weight had been a problem because he has been almost on the verge of kicking the bucket. "I want you to get out there and catch me this killer that takes eyes. Don't you see my eyes?" He said it with sarcasm, "I want you to go back out there and see what you can find at Debra Mancefield's house and bring me back something or don't come back without something hard on that person." He checked his pocket and looked for the pack of Marlboros full flavor 100s, Maddison knew he had been craving for one of them for the last 10 minutes as he moved his hand altough he had one already. Smokers and the need for their fix, she thought with amusement. Everyone had been a smoker in the 80s as everyone had been able to smoke wherever they wanted. "Captain…if you would like to have one, by all means." "Well, I have been cutting down to at least three packs a day, that's the only way I can keep my mind clear being in the goddamn crazy house!" His face bore an annoyance for how life had been as captain in the 22nd Precinct of Tampa's finest. Located in good old Carrollwood area. Not much of anything had been happening besides the usual burglaries and speeders. There had never been signs of any serial killer at work. The captain's hand twitched as he reached for a Marlboro cigarette that had been lost in the pocket. He had the jitters from not being able to sit down for 20 minutes and smoke. "Well, darn it!" The captain looked down at his pockets checking for any signs of a lighter. "Just my luck, today. My last cigarette and now this." Maddison thought, well if he was a woman, I don't think he could have dealt with having pms we have every month. She shook her head in disgust at the habit of his smoking blues. The areas had been littered with fast food wrappers from different places such as Pizza Hut, McDonald's and of course, Dunkin'. A favorite had been Dunkin' Donut's coffee as she had a full pot of coffee brewing on her desk, just in case she needed a cup of it. Her desk had a picture of her and her father when she had been about 12-years old. Time flew by when she thought about it. Many awards were crowded around her desk to show her skills in fire arms, arrest per city, as she lead the team in that. Not much stood in her way of life besides a man to care for her. Motherhood was in the future, she dreamt of that white- picket fence scenario that Carrollwood had to offer.

She was living at a small apartment overlooking the lake in the Forest Hill area. It was Lake Carroll to be exact. Life was all right, but the pressures of the new homicide in the Clearwater area had made things crazy. The Clearwater police had asked Captain McDonald to have his best person on the job as was the normal procedure when they could not handle that type of work. When Maddison went to school and graduated from the University of South Florida, she had taken her major in Psychology and had dealt with the criminally insane. Her mind told her that it had been an abused man of some kind that had daddy issues and also thought of the women of unfit mothers as maybe mothering types of his motherly insecurities as a man. But why did he take out the eyes, what is the correlation to it? She pondered it with her detective mindset. "Maddison! The captain brung her back to reality as he was not sure why she had been daydreaming. His eyes were like tiny balls of chocolate when he squinted when he was talking. "Come over here and I want to show you something," She had been on the job as a detective for the last couple of weeks.

They strolled through the Tampa police department, she was like a kid in a candy store. They passed the desk of the other police officer stations as theirs were just small cubicles in a small section of the station's of uniformed police officers. Computers were now the norm as everyone had access to the Commodore 64, which was a new innovation for 1982. As they came to the room where the door was painted red with the stenciled words "Authorized Personal Only" written on it. It had a code pad for when you could input the code as needed. A sign-in sheet was attached to the wall that read: Name, Date, Time and Signature of the person who wanted access. Only the captain and three other people had access to it.

"If you need something for your work, we have everything that pertains to your case." His face had a smile on it as he was about to give access to Fort Knox or something like it. He typed in the 4 digit code that was assigned to his person and kept track of the amount of times he had entered per day, over two would be a red flag.

She stood there in anticipation of what goodies stood in there. He gave her his wink that made her feel like he had given her the respect as a top of the line detective. The door crept open as if he wanted no one to hear them breaking in. He stopped in mid stride as he was about to let her in. "You have to take a lie detector test before you can enter this room." She stood their coolly as it was only one more step in becoming a bonafide detective for Tampa like her dad had been. The man that had killed him, had been in prison for the last 12 years. She had never visited him but he was not that far away as he was sent to Florida State prison in Gainesville to fry in Old Smoky. He had claimed he never killed him.

"I am just joking and, of course, we need our number one rookie to have access." The door opened as she saw what looked like a drug dealer's paradise with bags full of cocaine, she thought that Scarface would have been in all his glory in this room.

The metal shelves were about 5 feet tall in height and the width had been at least 10 feet in length. Her eyes caught to her left what had been a stack of cash that looked to be over at least a million of some form of drug dealer's currency that they once had. On the right had been a stock pile of every weapon that had been confiscated in different arrests in Tampa. She loved the double barrel shot gun that would put you out of your misery fast, if it had been used. He looked at her and waves his finger as to warn her, "If you need any of this, please sign out what you need." They had sat in there daydreaming about all the money, but as good cops, well, there was no taking to be honest.

"I want to introduce you to your new partner Stranz, you are going to work with detective Johnson, Milton Johnson, he has been on the force for the past 30 years. You will be like his Siamese twin. When he eats you will eat and when he shits you will take a shit! Do you copy that?" Maddison was well aware that she would not be working on her own and she had just been pushing papers and pens for the past two weeks.

Madison knew that Johnson was a man's man and a tough-as-nails cop that did not take shit from any other cops. He had over 10,000 arrests in his career as a detective and would retire this year.

"I want to introduce you to him now while I have you in my sights."

Detective Johnson was a black man in his late 50's, his hair had been a short but neatly trimmed afro, his mustache had also been cop regulation in length as he was not allowed to have a beard. He had been a pretty tall man being over 6 foot 3 inches tall. He had a southern accent having been born in the south of good old Georgia. He wore a black suit most of the times as he had it custom-made for him by the famous Ludwig Vance of South Tampa and if you had one of these custom suits, you had been lucky.

His desk was littered with lots pictures of perps that had been on the loose in the surrounding areas. "Detective Johnson this is your shiny new recruit Miss Stranz. Please take good care of her because your last one had quit the goddamn force!" The captain's face had an expression of a man trying to find his way with such a hardcore veteran as Johnson was.

"Yep send 'em my way, I send 'em back." He never knew who they were. Johnson did not like having young females on his roster because most of the time they could not handle his sense of humor.

Maddison put her hand out expecting a return handshake, but what she had gotten was a little rejection by Johnson. "Pull up a chair and let's get the formalities out of the way Missus Stranz!" Milton stared at her with malice, intent on making her quit on her first day together with him.

"OK, great and it looks like you two will be just fine." The captain had said in a sarcastic tone to level any tension. He left the two of them sitting face to face as two boxers were ready to toe off in a battle of the giants in Madison Square Garden. Now Maddison was not in any way scared as her veteran had showed the first move of the chess match.

Johnson picked up his morning brew and took a sip of scolding hot coffee, the steam resonated off of his lips. "I got three rules if we are working together...1, no being late and I mean at all, 2, come to work prepared and, 3, don't follow the other two and I will have you sent back from wherever you had been prior to this." Maddison stood up and saluted him like he was the General in the war. "I understand, sir!" "Ok, fine, and enough with antics Stranz." He had felt a smile come over him as he knew he had a rookie on his hands, but she might not disappoint him this time.

Milton looked outside and pointed to the car that was parked all by itself. Maddison could read the sign that was sitting directly in front of it. It read Milton Johnson VIP parking and under in smaller print, read 'don't park here or get a foot up in your ass' painted with spray paint in red. "Whoever did that will be dead when I catch his ass!" Maddison's face had a smile come on it as she could not control the foot up in your ass remark. The car that was parked there had been a 1982 corvette with a black paint job and it had the T-top to boot. The C3 was built in 1980 and it had been a retirement gift from the force to Milton to show their appreciation for his hard work. Brand new 1982 model was by far better than the previous years that had been in production.

"I am taking you out to lunch and you are buying." Now Johnson had a smile for once and Maddison had shook her head as an agreement for the gesture. They might be just right for each other Milton thought after all.

Chapter 4
Another kill

Brody drove Angie home as he had gotten done from the beach the two had been having fun at. The rain storm had come in fast and the lighting started to erupt as if the Gods were fighting.

She looks so good and I can't believe it, am I losing my mind. The fucking monster will come sooner than I like. I really wanted to keep this one.

Brody had felt the beast coming on him as he now needed his fix of blood. "Angie, tell me what you think about tonight and did you have fun?" She was making me feel very anxious and I couldn't stand it. I needed to get her out of here before I knocked her brains out. Yeah, my house is right this way. She had lived in a classy part of south Tampa and she had been loaded I thought. The streets were clean and almost seemed like a dream, it looked like a model neighborhood. They pulled up to the exclusive drive that lead into Lion Estates. The gate looked very prestigious and the lions were on each side of the opening of the gate which had been built high. It had been at least 10 feet I thought. Thank God, good thing the guard shack had been empty, so no track of any entry.

I wonder how much one of these houses would have cost, definitely more than I can afford. The notion was sure funny. "What type of work do you do?" I was staring into her eyes as she was willing to tell me. "I am an escort and you know finding me will cost a guy like you at least $300 for the night and I don't take checks." "What do you mean, I thought you really liked me as person," I had said and my face was blank as I know don't have any remorse for what I am about to do to this bitch. We sat there in her driveway, "Ok, let me get the money and it's over here." She was now smiling as she had seen my tone change to a John and she had no shame in her game. It would be funny to have my hammer in her head, I will wrap my hands and choke the life out of her breathing soul. The monster was here and he would need blood shed to go away happy. My mind always blanked out when he came into my soul like a bad itch that did not go away. He could be felt through my veins as they started to boil with heat, the smell was like sweet smells that light up nostrils with fragrance and best of all my strength was through the roof as I was now as strong as two of me. I would kill this bitch with pleasure. The monster grabbed her with full force strangling her life out, her eyes were popping out just like when you squeeze the stress ball that it reminded me of. Her hands grabbed mine with such force and cut me leaving my skin in her finger nails. The blood started pouring out like drops of tiny blobs of rain that blanketed the Ford van as the tan interior had now been tarnished with my blood. Her breath was slowly leaving her, her eyes shut as the monster sucked her soul out leaving a limp body to hang in the passenger seat. I felt nothing as she had used me for her greediness, my vision is now what do I do with the body. Her house was all alone and none of the neighbors have seen me. I need to take out her eyes as she has seen my soul and I can't have that. My trusty knife sat there like force of nature ready to use its power to take Angie's eyes out like a trophy almost. The scene had been set like a nightmare for the hooker and the last thing she would have thought would have been to be killed by the monster. I checked my watch and it was very late from hanging out with her. My arm had scratches in the right arm as the blood had been drawn. I started with the right eye pulling it out, sticking the knife in was like going through butter. The texture had been like well-done eggs that had overcooked. The smell was strange and almost like raw bacon mixed with iron. It almost made me gag. I had a small baggy that one would use to hold weed and I slipped in the eyes as it had been my second set of them that I would keep as a secret for me to have access to only. The other pair had been in my closet wrapped away in plastic wrapper in my upper dresser drawer where it had been kept so I could look at it, at any time. If someone found out and I would be thrown in the crazy house for the rest of my life. I want to bring her back and keep her at my house. But Dad would have to go, if he found out that would be the end of me. I need to get home before anyone catches me with this dead chick slumped over like a dead dog. I needed to put her in the back of the van to decide where I would put the body after.

The back had been a work-style van as I needed it to make the trips easier when I picked up some chicks for fun and decide who lives and who dies. I backed out in slow motion as the van had sounded loud as if the exhaust had a cutout that had made it noticeable from a distance. Her blue face had looked like a swimmer that had lost the battle to breathe with holes in the sockets. The night's air had been a little chilly as the dew was on the hood of the van. I started trying to get my mind back from the grasp of the monster. I have no idea why I killed another but my mind is simply fucked beyond repair. She had looked a certain way when her face is shown after death, their soul had been sucked out and eaten live. I have her eyes, it's now a collectable thing I guess like some killers would keep their wallets or purses but now I have four eyes and they don't see anymore.

The van had been a gore fest from the first murder. There had been a sheet that was the color of night as I would use it to conceal the body from prying eyes if I got stopped by any coppers around town. The body would have to be disposed of somehow and the other woman had been a pick-up from a bar in the beach area and it had been the same beach that Angie and I went to. How sweet, Angie and I could have been a lovely couple if it weren't for that evil monster controlling my mind like a cancer eating away my brain to mush.

I had covered the body as I wrapped it up like a pig in the blanket like our mothers made for us when we were just young and innocent.

I remember my mother coming in to tuck me in at night, every night and my dad had beaten her for not buying in his beer one night. I remember it clear as day now and it had been like my mind had forgotten it like a bad dream. Tony must pay for his sins of the world. My eyes squinting from the sheer joy of ending that piece of shit's life. Oh, the time has come to pay Tony a visit from the hammer fairy.

I watched him push her into the counter and he had lied to the police and said she had slipped on a puddle of water. I had been numb and could not even open my mouth to the police during that time. Now you would not be able to speak to anyone. "What is it, Tony? Cat's got your tongue." I sat there in the van laughing at the statement that I had just said to myself. Let's bring Tony a present tonight.

I drove the van heading back to good old Carrollwood with my new dead girlfriend in the back, oh, and disregard the pun if I do say so myself.

I had teased my hair back up to look like the badass punk rocker I was. I did like to look a lot like Billy Idol I thought as I glimpsed in the rear view mirror, just to catch myself. I had not been a fan of hurting anyone and I don't know why I changed and did a 360 in acting. I had to try to get a hold of myself before it happens again. My mind raced as I caught a black and white behind me as the lights flashed red and blue as the strobe lights hit like the clubs atmosphere. The young man with the big hat comes up to me like he is asking for my autograph.

Why did he pull me over? I didn't notice anything about why I got pulled over. I can see the dead body behind me as the night's sky.

The officer is a rather fat man and I can see by his name tag that it said Reggie as the last name. His eyes are brown like a shit turd in the toilet bowl. His hair a short crop of cut as you can imagine for a cop, looking the same as they all do. "License and registration, young man?" His voice had a southern twang to it as he was from the Deep South, maybe Plant City. "Why did you pull me over, Officer Reggie?" Well, your back taillight is out on the left side. You have rather dark tint there and that's against the law. My eyes saw the 38 on his hip and I know if I go to take on this cop, that I might be taken. My hammer is in the back and it's my only shot if I want to make it out alive. Or they might send me to the crazy house, if he sees the body laying in some old black sheet with blood stains on it with the missing eyes. They would put me to death in the chair that is referred to as Old Smoky in the Florida State prison, where some of the worst of the worst are. "Come out of your van and come see what I am taking about."

The cop had pointed toward the back as he went ahead of me like cattle going to the slaughter house to be butchered. My hammer was in my waistband and strapped to me like a knight with his sword ready for battle. As he turned toward me with the last bit of life he had left. Whack! As I cracked it right through is forehead and killing him on impact. His brains were hanging out like Christmas decorations for the vanity of it. His body hung on to the side of the van as he tried to catch his balance before he took a nasty fall.

I looked over my shoulder to see if anyone was coming, it had been quiet as a mouse roaming around and not letting the owners of the houses see anything. His body must have been 300 pounds of pure fat. I opened the van doors wide to see if I could fit the double bodies in and now I was dead and I had no way out of this nightmare. I could not get out of this, as the body count had climbed to the top in 1982 of three.

Chapter 5
The Body Shop gym

The morning had been full of rain as God had sent his water to feed his plants for the day. The news had said that the weather was not going to clear up much on the fact that a tropical storm had come in from the Gulf of Mexico.

The alarm went off with the old-fashioned ringing of the two bells that had annoyed Maddison for the last two years as a cop. "I need to sleep, give me break!" She had shouted at some make believe bad guy trying to wake her out of her beauty sleep. She had been a bad sleeper and had to take sleeping pills just to get through another night as a cop.

Now being the rookie of the year had its perks with any good job done. It was a status she had to keep up as a diehard detective.

Life was very different now from the last two weeks that had given Maddison Stranz nightmares of the woman with spooned-out eyes, it crept her out like a weird macabre ritual for the New Year. No one had every done this as a serial killer, more or less, a sick person in the sense of it. She thought about the pictures of the victims as she hung them up in her bedroom. Well, didn't all good cops study their work? Even when they slept.

Maddison shook her head as she was now awake and that today was her day off. She had an appointment at the new gym down the road off of Dale Mabry Highway. Well, it was either that one or the more expensive Gold's Gym. Her pay as a detective was 15,000 dollars, pay for the 80's, and was not that bad for a single woman living in the greater Tampa Bay area.

She sat up like a zombie awakening from a centuries old sleep. Her eyes were bloodshot after tossing and turning throughout the night. "Maybe if…a man would fuck me good…I could have slept finally like a baby!" She had said with her most sarcastic voice for this time of the morning. It was not unusual for a woman 25 years old, to have a super sex drive, but, she needed a partner to keep her in line at home as a good woman. Hell, she had made enough money as a detective, now to cover two people living in the modern times of the new America, where woman worked as much or more than a man.

Maddison got out of bed and her body was tight from running and doing weight training for her job. She had placed 3rd in the mile run out of the 50 or so recruits.

She wore her favorite black panties that read super chick on the back she had gotten from a past lover. Jon or Jonathon Rutgers had been a man's man and a super workout partner at the Body Shop gym, but he had gotten one of the girls pregnant at the gym in the men's bathroom. She had been not as pretty or even as fit as Maddison, but sometimes men can't keep their dicks in their pants long enough not to cheat, she thought with an angry sigh.

Maddison's room was in her tiny shit hole of an apartment that had been very rough as it was on discount from the woman she rented it from. The rent had been $300 a month with everything included to boot. The place had been very messy and had the same fast food wrappers that had been at her desk in the 22nd Precinct. Her bed had filled up her bedroom as she had loved a big comfy bed, but no one to keep her company. "Might just get my ass into the dating game." She told herself as she raised her arms with a whatever feeling.

Time to get some grub but I can't take another fast food meal for breakfast. Might just make a protein shake and slam it before the workout, she thought to herself.

She had been in killer shape for all the junk she had eaten as a cop. It never got better for food as a detective and her fellow police officers had shown her the way of bad habits for the morning's sweet coffee and several doughnuts. Ring, Ring, her dial phone had rung as she had made an appointment with the gym today. Maddison reached for the phone with swift finger that grabbed it as the last ring had occurred with a "Hello, Stranz residence." She spoke to the willing Brody. "I wanted to call you up and just confirm for your appointment with me?" Maddison had not been sure, but it had sounded like the big beefy guy that kept hitting on her like a stalker. "I am not that desperate." "Your appointment is at 9am and I will be training you for our introduction to fitness goals, it's a program for new gym members." Madison had been tired still, but she had to keep on going like a tiger ready to pounce on the running antelope. "Ok, I will see you up there in a few hours," she had said to Brody."

Maddison had made breakfast, after all, of eggs to give her some juice for the workout with Brody. Maddison had been in her gear as she had the look of someone ready for war.

The heaps of garbage littered the sidewalks of the residential neighborhood in the Forest Hills area. She had grown up here as she had lived in Tampa her whole life. Not much had been going on around this area except for the pigs that trashed it.

She had saved up, quit some money over the years to have a new car that had been the love of her life. She had not been able to resist the 1982 Trans Am that had been her favorite since the TV show "Knight Rider", which had been shown on all of the cable TV stations to show-case such a badass car. It had all the bells and whistles that had cost her the extra money for such a studly car. "If only my boyfriend had been this sexy," she thought with a giggle that came out of her. Or he might be intimidated by a cop and her sports car? She was set, as she was leaving and heading off to the Body Shop gym for her training session with Brody, her stalker, typical meathead jock, his penis must have been tiny to make up for all that muscle. Chuckle.

The time was 9am as she pulled in the parking lot of the Body Shop. With a rumbling of the big V8 that could be heard around the block and back. She was ready for her appointment with Brody, but she hoped he would not hit on her like a crazy man in heat. The Body Shop had been a hole-in-the-wall place and if you did not know what it was, then you wouldn't know it was even a gym. The color of the gym had been blue with a trim of an ordinary white trim of the building that was attached to a video store called Rent-A-Movie that Maddison had ventured into on many lonely nights, as she had been all alone eating popcorn and watching some random chick flicks on the VHS player. She had been lucky to have won a VHS player from the local Radio Shack with an entry for the drawing that she had won by luck, one of those had gone for over $1,000 dollars brand new.

Hardly any of the windows could be seen in the gym, like it was a secret hangout for the anonymous person that wanted to build a nice physique. She had walked up with her gym bag in hand and a protein shake for the workout. She opened the door and inside had been many varieties of cold iron being lifted like toy weights. Many of the men and woman had been working out like they were trying to gain a perfect physique for the 80's. The new fad had been using performance-enhancing drugs to gain the edge on the workout game. Even one of the greats had entered the gym, he had won the Mr. Olympia title countless times.

Many names were scribbled with dates and pictures next to them like an autograph session for the famous. "Oh my God and that's the guy that keeps hitting on me." Maddison knew that it had to be him that she would get, she frowned. He had creeped her out many times as he had come over for the small talk about weird things that did not make any sense for what was going on in the gym. He had always dressed like the guys she had found very attractive and would not have been a great boyfriend material for a future with. Either they did not care about her and just devoted themselves on their appearances. That was the young beefy hunks of the era.

"Hey, Maddison!" Brody had called from one of the machines as he had been pumping iron like a bodybuilder trying to inflate his muscles. He had one earring of a cross in his ear and the blond-punked hair that had reminded her of a twin of Billy Idol to which she had been appalled as to why she had found him so attractive. Brody ran up as he was prepared for the meeting like a professional stalker. He knew she had a Trans Am and it had been a black one that had the big V8 unlike his V6 Firebird. His insecurities had run rampant from the sheer thought of his car being the weaker model.

I have some water for you as I know you have been drinking this brand. It had been strange she had never showed him the water she had liked to drink called "Party in the 80's- themed" water that could only be found at Albertson's grocery on Waters Avenue near her house.

He presented it to her like a diamond ring to show his affection for her. She knew he had a crush on her for sure as he had been so kind to her and most men did not even offer to pay for dinner now a days. Thanks she said with a smile of a lady that had been spoiled by the trainer. "I am so glad you made it and you look the part of an athlete," he had said to her. He stood close to her as he was in kissing distance and Maddison backed up to gain some space from the overly excited Brody.

"As you know, this is the place to come for the most intense workouts that we can offer for the beginner or to the advanced cliental.

They trained long and hard for the next hour. Maddison was beat and Brody had put it on her hard like a vise grip, her body was wet from the intense workout.

They had been in the stretching room and Maddison was laying on her back, the tension was getting a little high as he was stretching her leg muscles out as it had been a leg day workout that she would feel it tomorrow and even felt it now. The time had shown 10am and Maddison still had the rest of the day to enjoy.

"You did a hell of a good job today." He was stretching near her vagina and it was getting hit as this beef cake was making her horny from the stretching. They both had the feeling like some form of sex would take its toll on the two. "I would like to take you out some time, Maddison." The weirdness all of a sudden had gone away like she was starting to feel him now. "I...am pretty busy for dating, to be honest and that is saying lightly Brody" and

Maddison was feeling apprehensive about how he had asked her out and even that he was at work. "Well, if you want to know, we could have a meal together and it's my treat," she had said in a school girl's approach to love. "Well, I will take you up on that Maddison, for sure, and you know my number." She had winked at Brody with a playfulness to it. "Well, it's a date then and we will have a good time and I can assure you that." Brody had seemed like a real gentleman. It was strange at how he had changed from the weird stalker to a real romantic. His hand went to reach to let her up. I will walk you to your car, Maddison. They had walked outside towards her car as he had noticed the Trans Am in person. "So we will meet up in the next couple of days for our date," Brody said with clear understanding of the date. Brody went in for the kiss as Maddison did not resist it.

"That was nice." She had said to the serial killer. It would be her worst nightmares as the monster would need the new blood again, soon and Maddison would be his most valuable price because he wanted her eyes.

Chapter 6
Father knows best

The room was a bloody mess as I had brung back the eyes from Angie. She had been a heavy girl weighing over a buck fifty of boobs and ass. Her body had been a good piece to look at when she had been alive and healthy a couple nights ago. I wish I had not killed her and could have at least taken her out, "You fucking idiot, she was a prostitute!" I had been shouting out in frustration. "What are talking about, shut the fuck up!" My dad had been yelling at me from his coma room, from the pills and beer, which made him a lush and that was a sin in my book.

"Dad,...you would not understand...leave me alone!" "Brody get your ass over here right this goddamn minute before I..." I held the bag of eyes like a prize as it was the last thing that they had looked at in the brief moment before their souls were the monsters to keep. He came out as the victims were near, like a blood-thirsty creature of the night.

My body had changed from a man to some form a beast and every time I blacked out as the world had eaten me up in the black hole or the abyss.

My room had my special place as I had my rock posters on the wall and my bloody movie posters. Ted Bundy had been my role model for all the killings he had done. I need not think he was the greatest because I had more kills after a while. I had my hammer as my choice weapon for all of my victims and one good shot to the head would be the kill shot.

The cop and the hooker had been laid together as the monster had strung them up and I had saw it through his eyes, he was pure evil and I had two minds now for what reason I had no clue. Life had the strangest things happen. I had cut his eyes out and feed it to him, down his piggy throat with pleasure.

Angie's house had been the place where I showed his work as if they were a flag hanging in the wind. Like a kite flying high for everyone to see. The news would have the story as the lead story in the surrounding areas. He had smeared the blood and wrote a nice message for cops when they would find them together. Lions Estates would be remembered for the two killings of the hooker and the pig. Both had the monster's trademarks.

Daddy had been asleep peacefully in his hospital bed with beer cans and liquor bottles laying around like an alcohol junkyard. The TV had been playing the nightly news and Channel 8 had the top story for the 20th of February. The reporter sat there stunned as the story went, "Two murdered in cold blood! Last night the two victims, 21-year old Angie Valente and a police officer, both from the Clearwater area, had been brutally killed and their eyes missing." His face was as white as a ghost from the story as it had been a strong case for one of deadliest killings in recent history. "As soon as we have an update in this double homicide, we will bring them to you from your news source." As the screen had turned and the American anthem began playing for the TV to end the night's programming.

I had felt so tired as my body had not had a good night's sleep in sometime. After I take care of the old bastard, then I could take a nap and get some rest, but the monster was ready to come for his next victims. I had my knife ready and in my pocket as the blade was about five inches in length and it had a naked chick showing her big boobs with pleasure. She would pierce his heart and the pain would go away, like a bad dream. The monster would want his blood soon and I could feel it as my skin burned and I could feel bones shifting in my body like a rattle snake moving. The blood would need to be drunk to gain the most intense feeling, he had shown me this in my mind as he had done before.

I tucked my knife in my back pocket as I was ready for the killing of Tony Bransford. His eyes would be in the bag or maybe the monster would make him eat it, like his supper. My face had no reaction from the thoughts that I was supposed to have, like sympathy for him, and he would see it soon enough.

"Look at me, Tony!" My eyes burning with pain. His eyes looked somewhat as scared as a mouse caught by a cat. "You know I know you are a killer! I saw you kill mom as you shoved her to the countertop like a rag doll. I was too young and stupid!" My finger pointed at him as he was a trapped animal in a cage. "What are you taking about, boy?! You better get your finger out of my face!" Tony sat up shirtless, his face was red as a red stop sign. His eyes closing in on me as he thought he had the upper hand. "You have one more chance to come clean." I had given him a chance to tell the truth before I ended his fucking life. I reached for my knife from my back pocket and showed him what he will get if he does not cooperate with me. I flicked the knife open as the blade shone in the lamp's light. Tony's face was a mess, as he started. "I only killed one that I had meant to kill and it had started back when you was just 12 and I had been out and working. I had shot a cop and ripped his throat out like an animal and I loved the taste of blood. Now I know where you get it from. He had died at the scene as he had written me a ticket and I framed a fucking guy, Victor Cruz...All I knew was that he had taken the blame for my crime. And he had a 12-year old girl about your age, that fucking cop. So what, I had killed." He had spit at me with an evil laugh, he had no remorse for what he had done. He was now a killer like me. My face started hurting as the monster was coming to life. I fell to the ground with a thump. Tony looked to see where I went. As I stood up and my eyes were red as I had grown in size for some strange reason. I could see myself this time and I had looked very evil and it was not something I had ever seen in my life until tonight. I started stabbing him over and over until his body looked like a pin cushion. His eye were out and now the evil Tony had been killed for the shit that he had done to me and my mom.

The transformation had been very painful and it was not like a muscle pain when you worked out hard, but the muscles had mutated and became larger, about twice the size of my already 20-inch arms. The monster needed to kill as he grew when he took souls. The new chick would be next if I did not keep him away from Maddison.

Chapter 7
The blood bath sign

The morning after the gym workout with her personal trainer had gone real well compared to when he had been a real weirdo in the past like the plague that had killed thousands of people back in the day. The hangover had been bad from last night after a wild night of drinking and throwing up all night due to alcohol consumption. Her eyes came to the light as the sun's rays were shining bright in its morning glory.

"Ring, ring," the phone was blowing off the hook like a fucking wakeup call from hell. Maddison had looked at breaking it to tiny pieces because it was Saturday morning and she did not have a shift until tomorrow night. She had wanted to sleep-in since she did not sleep from the partying and the throwing up combo. "Helllooooo," she had answered in a sleepy tone that had not sounded like herself. "Wake up, there's something you need to see." Said her new partner, Johnson. He had sounded like something bad had taken place. "Where should I meet you? Today is my day off." Maddison still had her party dress on from last night and as she looked down her heels were on the bed. Fuck. I don't remember any of this, she had thought to herself. As she pulled the phone down from her ear like a kid trying to get away from punishment. "We had a problem the other night as some neighbors had called it in to the Clearwater police. You know damn well that they can't even find their asses if one put it in their faces," Johnson said. He had been telling the truth as they did not have any good detectives that could handle a case like this. He read "the monster strikes again and takes eyes from victims." It came from the local paper. He had been in shock as he had read the newspaper from today. "So get your gear on and meet me at the station in 20 minutes. Oh and don't be late, you know what I said about it in my rules." She had known the stupid rules would show their ugly heads at her soon enough, but shit, at the butt crack of dawn. It was 7am and she had fallen asleep around 4am. I am still a little drunk and better get some black coffee ASAP, she thought.

The office had been pretty busy as the men and women made their rounds. The offices had pretty much everyone there. They were answering phones and taking tips and statements from the "serial killer on the loose" scenario. Maddison had come to the coffee station, a make shift desk that had a coffee pot and cups on the regular.

The white sign in magic marker had read, [If you finished the coffee, please make another] and under it someone had scribbled in, [Johnson will put a foot up in your ass!] It was funny how this guy Johnson controlled the whole station or at least the guys had made it a point to put it in print at the parking lot and now the coffee area. She shook her head chuckling silently.

As Maddison looked up from her sleepy feeling, her eyes saw a black guy that was Johnson in a crisp black suit with perfectly polished shoes with a brilliant shine. Wow, he dresses like the FBI, Maddison had thought when she saw the neatly dressed Milton Johnson standing in front of her crossing his arms. "Well, 19 mins and counting, good, you are a punctual one." "Well, you know a lady needs some time to get ready." He puckered his lips like a duck from the aggravation of this 'wet behind the ears' recruit. Time would tell if Miss Thang could handle the Commander of the detectives.

"Shit you smell like a vodka and I am trying to be polite. Go get yourself some mouth-wash and freshen up!" You have one minute to get back here at attention, rookie." Maddison knew she had to impress him at all cost and even if he was a pain in her ass, well, sometimes you had to kiss some ass in this life. "Ok, sir!" As she spoke she had stood tall and saluted him as if he was the General in the military. He had also liked the feeling of the salute. He had noticed that Maddison's pant suit had some left over stains and that was going to be her ass if she did not get it together soon. As she walked away, the only words that came out were, "These dang rookies are going to give me a heart attack."

As Maddison had returned from her little freshen-up, she had been looking for Johnson. Well, this man is something else, she thought. She walked over by the window facing his spot. It was his black corvette with him sitting in the passenger seat. As Maddison walked up and hopped in, her face had been flustered as her olive skin tone had turned a bright red from the annoyance from her new partner. "You are not riding in here." "Are you serious?" She asked in a pissed off tone. "First you call me on my day off and got me here. You know 20 minutes is not long enough and then you left me waiting like an ass in the hall!" She had raised her tone at him for the first time. "Oh, now you got some balls as he pointed the finger at her." "Ok I get it, most cops or wannabe cops can't handle me because I tell it like it is. Anyway, let's get moving and like I said you are buying breakfast." "No, you owe me, sir." They sat there in silence as they had decided that talking had hit them no where right now. Johnson thought, she might just make it after all.

They made a stop at the famous, 'Mom's and Sons - All You Can Eat Breakfast' diner that had been a favorite of Maddison's since she was just a young girl visiting with her father. The building had been a 50's dinner, it was a big white building with the checkerboard that had been there for the last 13 years. As they walked in Maddison had recognized one of the ladies that had been serving the place for the past 30 years, she had looked to be about 80 and had a blossom, full of wrinkles as she had tried to cover them up with makeup. Her hair had been in a bun as she had bright red hair as the white hair had taken the color and made it very bright. The inside was also very busy as the restaurant had been moving at the speed of light, The decor had been white and checkered with red booths that had amplified the 50's era. Milton had looked like he was not enjoying the atmosphere due to it being something not fitting his caricature. "Well, would you two lovebirds be dining in or taking out?" Milton had looked at her name tag that had read Betty. "By the way, we are not a couple," He had rolled his eyes as he had said that to Betty. Betty had two menus, she lead them toward their lover's lair. "Take it easy on the old lady," Maddison had been letting him know that she was just getting old and when she saw a man and a woman together, it would most likely be a relationship in Betty's eyes.

The booth had been very clean and not one crumb was seen on the table. "Now you two have a sit, right?" As the two laid into the booth with discomfort from the lover's remark. "I am starved!" Said Maddison with a smiled as she look at Johnson. "Well, did yous all make a decision, yet?" As Betty was back with her pen and pad.

"Freeze, motherfuckers!" As two masked men were wearing ski masks blasted their way in. "Get down on the ground, before I blow each one of you a new asshole!" He had shouted out with fury. They had jumped on the table as they were waving two sawed off shot guns at the customers. Maddison and Johnson were under the table, "You packing?" As Milton had asked her with seriousness into his statement. Maddison had got very close to Milton's face. She lifted up her shirt and showed a 38 Special that had been her dad's before. "I am gong to take them down with you or without you, Miss Stranz." Maddison's heart had been racing laps around the Indianapolis 500. Maddison looked and had seen them facing away. Maddison had gotten up from under the table. "You two drop em or I am going to stop you. With deadly force!" She had been waving her hand at the would-be robbers. "Fuck you!" As her partner got out from the table. Pulled out his police-issued 9mm Glock that had his initials embossed with a traditional MJ. One shot fired from the Glock towards the fat one with the black sky mask on, the bullet proceeded at the speed of light pumping that 9mm bullet straight into his head with the casing flying to the ground. It had been like a slow motion movie like one of the Hollywood movies as the heroine kills the bad guy at the end to save the day. His brain splatter had poured out from the front part of his head like a fountain of gore spraying his partner in crime.

The skinny one had his gun locked and loaded as he pumped one of the triggerful blasts into Milton's head giving a chain reaction. As Maddison ducked down the bullet missed her by a half of a foot. She was one lucky woman, but her partner was now a corpse as had been the other robber. The man dropped the weapon as Maddison had aimed to kill him. In a killer stance that she was known for when she was in the police academy a few years ago.

"Put your hands on your head or you are a dead motherfucker!" She had looked at Milton and checked his pulse to see if any life was left, it had been a long career for him as now he could rest in peace for his after life. She had felt sadness in her heart and this bad guy would pay dearly for killing a cop.

Maddison went to the bad guy like a hawk, she had her cuffs on her hip, she slapped them on with authority squeezing his wrist to chase some deep bruising. The crowd had been stunned as two bodies were dead. It had been a nightmare for everyone to view.

Maddison had checked him for any more weapons or drugs. Nothing more had been found. "What's your name? You piece of trash!" She was angry like a mad woman ready to kill her prey. "I want a lawyer!" the skinny one demanded as that was going to save his life from old smoky. "Where you are going, they don't have anything good for you!" Max McBride was on his driver's license. She pulled off the mask and the face had been more like a nightmare as his face was tattooed, with his whole face as a fucking skull and the eyes were black circles, it was not his costume, but a real full-blown tattoo. He should have been in a horror movie. "Why did you do it?" Maddison had grabbed him by his shirt, so she could get him up. The other cops were now pulling up, one of the cops had checked on Maddison and it had been one of her friends from the force. Cassie Benton had come up to check on Madison. Cassie was the type of cop that had followed the rules, she was the kind of beauty that would have knocked any of the boys dead. Her hair had been a sexy pinup style as her red locks had been colored bright red. She had been a rather muscular girl as she worked out at the Body Shop gym where Maddison had also been introduced from. "Oh my, girl, I would not have expected you to have been here!" Cassie's face had been in shock as she had known both Milton and Maddison from the 22nd Precinct, the town was smaller than they all thought. Cassie looked at the robbery offender as he stood there in a zone, more than a killer, he had been on PCP or some other form of hard drugs. Cassie looked at Maddison and saw the gore that was attached to her clothes like a death note that was meant for her. She shook her head with an uneasy feeling. "Let's get this scum out of here before I blow his brains out or whatever remains from the drug use." Max McBride said to the two ladies with an evil speech, "I would have killed you with passion, bitch, and ate your guts for breakfast and then I would have fucked your friend." He snarled like a beefy dog trying to intimidate his prey. The tattoo had been extra scary as the monster looked like a monster and not just playing the part like some Halloween punk. He spat at them with such grossness and goo, that it landed on Cassie's face and the excess had hit Maddison like an acid rain from hell.

Wham! Her fist collided full force. Cassie's hand had knocked some teeth out from the forceful blow of the sick sounding destruction of teeth coming out like mar-balls. His mouth started bleeding as the flow of blood began pouring out. It had been unexpected. Some of the other officers had seen it and looked away as the man had deserved the justice that had followed.

The man had been knocked out like a title fighter and the last shot had knocked the champ out cold. Cassie had grabbed the bloodied man with one hand pulling him up by his cuffs, like a toy man. "Get this piece of trash outta here now!" She screamed at one of the rookies. The man would be booked in the 34th Precinct jail to await his murder sentencing charge that would follow soon after like a death sentence for killing a cop and robbing the restaurant.

The criminal had been led off and stuck in one of the police cruisers as was the standard practice.

"Shit I forgot to read him his rights! But it should not matter because no one likes a cop killer."

It was still part of her job to get to the site where the murder had taken place of the girl and the cop that had lost his life on the job. But now the stress of losing her partner would take her off of the job for a bit so she could regain her composer for her work or maybe forever. "I need to get home and get a shower and get this goddamn blood off me before I blow chunks all over the place!" Cassie knew the stress from the mental breakdown that had come from this horrible situation. They both looked at poor Milton Johnson, 30 years on the force and was close to retiring, but now was sent out of this life in a body bag.

Chapter 8
A killer's work is never done

My dad's head had stood there like a trophy and all the beatings that I had received from this evil man made me more than happy as he had died. His head up there, had been an amazing feeling as I had now had been a killer and could never go back to the world before the monster had gotten a hold of me this year and the Year of the Monster would be one to remember more than Bundy or other would-be killers of the past.

I stood there in all my glory, naked, as one would be and I loved how the blood felt as I took my shower with the new soap and drank his soul. I could feel their souls as one feels their stomach full. I closed my eyes and thought of that girl, Maddison and I had to have here. She would never know what I really did in my spare time. But her red-headed friend, Cassie, would be next on the agenda for the monster would need more blood as he would need to kill more people as the weeks turned into months and then years. Yes, I would claim another as he needed. Oh shit, the sound of the door bell had scared me as I jumped up from the bed with a sudden jolt coming down my body, I had to get cleaned up as it was almost too surreal for me. I don't feel I am a serial killer. Life just gave you lemons and then you made lemonade.

As I made my way over to the blinds to see what all that ringing had been. The cops had been there and it seemed to had been more than what I had expected. The lights had flashed as they were pulling my eyes in and I could not object from them. I needed to answer the door because I knew they were there to take me in. I had washed my face and the blood had washed off as the bad dream of forgotten souls had drained.

The monster would love to come out and kill these cops that had come for us, and I do mean us, because Brody was one and the monster had made his own mind the monster's now. I made my way through the house from my chambers to the front door as the red door would lead me to the four cops that were there. "Hello," I said through the peephole. "Is Brody Bransford there," the one cop with glasses had called from the outside. "Yes, it's he, how can I help you?" "We need to ask you some questions downtown. We can do this the easy way or you are not going to like the other way." "Ok, I am opening the door," I turned the handle as slow and steady so the cops would not shoot me through the door. "Put your hands up and walk back towards me slowly…lower your hands where I can see them and no funny business!" I did what the police officer had said. He had guided me to the police car with a powerful grasp. He had pushed my head in and started reading me, the Miranda Rights before they took me to the 22nd Precinct for my murder booking.

As I entered it, well aware that they did not have anything on me and I did not believe I did anything wrong as the monster was in charge of the killings. "Sit down and we will be right in to interview you." The detective had told me. The room had been what I had seen on TV and it was very depressing as a man like me should not be wasting his time in a hellhole like this. The desk had been bare to the bone, besides one of the ashtrays that had a cop car as the base for it. The windows had been shut with no view from the outside. It took about 45 minutes for the coppers to come back and talk to me about the two murders that had taken place on February 25th. As I see it a man in his early 40's with grey in his mustache had sat down in front of me like a real 1920s hard ass. He had on one of the old Italian gangsters pin-strip suits with a red bow tie and the matching hat to match. "Why am I here? You have no right to bring me here! I demand a lawyer and I have my rights as a citizen of this country, Dick Tracy!" I was furious that they had taken me out of my house cleaning and that meant the bodies that stood there like the decaying corpses that they were. "Water or a smoke?" The officer had pulled out tactics and from what I know, never take the free stuff. "No!" I said to him knocking the water to the floor. The water flew all over the place. Wham! The fist piled into my face knocking me to the floor with one punch like a heavyweight boxer. He picked me up like a drunken man had taken a fall. I grabbed my face, it hurt like a motherfucker. "Ok, I'm sorry, what do you want from me, man!" "I am going to record you now and if you don't want to talk, we will get you a lawyer. Would you be needing that lawyer now son, or after they are about to fry your ass?" His eyes bore into me, like a man possessed by evil. He squinted with his dark eyes that looked into my soul. "Yeah, give me one." "Ok, ok, you will be booked on murder charges, Brody Bransford!" "Whats your name? I am so happy you know mine."I had given a shot back as he was not going to kick my ass and take me out of the box. "I am your worst nightmare, son. My name is Jesse Lee and that's a name you won't forget now, will you?" He sat there in the leather seat as he rocked back and forth like an old grandpa trying to put himself in a comfortable spot. "Yeah, Lee," kiss my ass I thought, cops were like rodents and they needed to be exterminated like rats that roamed the streets, looking to eat anything.

It had been hours as I lay in my cell and it had been hot as no a/c. The bars had a metal base and no getting out from them. Some writings had been written in like tattoos of the previous men or crazies that had stayed here before. It had been a waiting game, the sounds from the other rooms were like screams from men being murdered. This holding cell had been rather small and claustrophobic. As I recalled the 3 or 4 other cells had been right next to each other. The concrete had been a divider from the other maniacs that were at the 22nd Precinct. I knew one of chicks that had been to my gym, shit she even had a thing for me as we kissed after our session. If she found out, well it might as well be my last time kissing her before being thrown in with the other killers.

"Bransford, you have a lawyer here for you, should I send her in?" The muscular guard had asked me from the front of my bars. I was not sure if they were fucking with me. "Yeah, send her in." The chair had sat in front of my cell and it was not very secure to talk to anyone. If I get out and I will, I will murder the people that had fucked with me. I had been losing my mind. the monster wanted to come out. It was always a problem when he needed bloodshed. This young 20-something, wet-behind-the-ears lawyer had strolled in, she had been right out of law school. Her look was attractive as her hair had been in a bun with very little makeup on. Her thin frame had fit nicely under her suit. I was not sure she was going to be able to handle this, but it was worth a try. "My name is Ava Taylor and I am your public defender from the Public Defender's office and I wanted to say that you are my first case." "Hmm, the point is, I did not do this and you got to believe me, Miss Taylor!" I was physically upset like I had been framed by some killer that had taken over my body. "I have been possessed by the demon monster. I am going to tell you how it got me, an evil entity took over my body and mind.

It all started in the beginning of this year, I had bought enough junk in my life that was more or less crap and did not make me feel better about myself. I sat there in my room, just another regular day in my life. But, this day, I had found a board game that had numbers and letters on it. My curiosity had gotten the better of me. To be honest, I had not believed in this kind of thing called black magic or whatever comes from unknown portals. As I recalled, there had been a moon on one side and sun on the other. The room had been pitch black as the book that had come with it. The old pawn shop had sold to me that very same day. It's weird how you did not come for such a thing. I had been looking for some VHS tapes, but this combo had stood out like something in a suspense novel. The book was just unknown if you were to look at. It had the same symbols like the board had on it. So I got it for 10 bucks. As I read this book of curiosity, well, the room had been blacked out with only several candles lined up to see what the hell would happen next. I put my fingers on this thing that I could move by pushing it, but the book had told me not to move and let the spirits take over. They could have been something demonic or good-hearted, you were not certain what would come next. I asked..'will I become rich' and that had been the turning point. The room swirled with red smoke coming from thin air, it had been like the New Year's fireworks had just blown off, several of them. My heart started to beat faster as it happened, I thought it would have pounded out of my chest. My eyes danced, looking around like a mad man. The heads of screaming demons floated above my head.

As I recalled..my hands felt glued on, they were not coming off unless I cut them off with an axe. It started to move as it spelled out 'demon monster.' My eyes rolled in the back of my head and my body floated off the floor several feet above, my head flew back as the spirit of the evil entity had been sucked in and I flew to the ground passing out for the rest of the night. As I woke up and saw that it must have been a dream, but I felt the effects of the demon in me. It's real and I never killed anyone and you got to believe me and get me out of here...fast!" I was totally out of breath from the distress of the demon story.

She had sat there concentrating on me like she was unsure if I was real or not. She looked into her purse and pulled out a smoke, she lit up a Newport and sucked in the nicotine like she was sucking in all of the air that had stood out there for Ava to take in. The smoke filled the room. She had looked nervous from the story with demonic spirts floating around. "Most likely you will have to use the insane defense," she had added to my case now. I sat there in disbelief that a spirit had inhabited my body, consuming my soul as a gateway to becoming a monster in the real form and wiping me out for good. I sat there on my bed, my stomach hurting like hell from the intense twisting in my stomach. I never knew I would be facing the electric chair, the only ones that would be there, would be the ghosts of the monster's murders. Hell house, take me now, I thought. My muscles twitched as my nerves started eating at me like worms crawling inside of my body. I was becoming evil and how could I go back, but the monster would become alive in 1982 as it had with me. "What do they have on me now?" I had asked with deep concern and had my fate coming down for the electric chair. I was thinking like a man and not the evil creature lurking inside like a beast from hell attacking anyone in his path. He must have killed women, was my feeling, as the victims had been prostitutes and also one cop that tried to stop him. I was not sure about my dad and why? I felt no remorse for that one as he had been a bastard and tormented me and had killed, as he told me of the horror story about the cop, he had made a man live his life in prison. She looked at me with a smile as she had something that could leave me in a good spot to get out of this prison. Her lips were moving and had not made a sound in my ears as sound had not come but just muffled sounds. She came closer to the cage as she pressed her lips close, but not close enough, she tried to make contact but nothing came out.

As the sound popped back like a swift punch to my gut, my eyes opened as my mind became alive. I was not in control as the great man that had lived a long time ago had become part of my soul. I could see his motive as he stalked the women of the night with a long hammer he carried around in his coat pocket and a knife to cut the eyes out, picking them off like flies on shit. Wham, the sound smashing through their head at will and hearing their cries of agony as he takes their eyes out, ripping their souls out to feed his evil soul. I could see the cars as they were model Ts and also the Spanish flu had just ended as the sick were all dead. The guards rushed in as he was on the ground playing coy to lead them in like cattle awaiting to be slaughtered for the hungry killer to make his move. My vision is above my head with not much light or hearing, but I am floating high as a kite. I see a name as it appears before me like a valid sign, the words omitted were...Vincent "The Monster" Grady. He had lived in the 1920s, murdering woman at will, He had killed over two dozen woman until he was caught in 1929. He was caught, about to kill his twenty-first victim. He had been put to death in the electric chair as he was one of the most evil men to ever live among us. Never play with evil objects that transfer the dead spirts to the living. As I am now possessed by the most evil entity known in this world...The Monster.

Chapter 9
Maddison's nightmares

Maddison had been at home ever since Milton had been killed in front of her eyes. Her mind had been reliving the homicide, like a bad dream that never went away. The blood smell had stuck to her as she smelt worn as day and night. He was a good man and his time had been cut short by the skull man. She laid in bed on leave for the incident and was coming back.

She tossed and turned as his face was etched in her mind like a burning fire growing as more gas was thrown on for more flames to shoot up.

Her eyes opened as her pupils grew, her thoughts pounded at her like flesh-eating cancer. Her breath was heavy as she came to with a cold sweat covering her naked body. Clothes were not an option during the night, it happened for the last couple days she thought. She looked over at the bell alarm clock, it had read 3am as the devil's hour had just come to be. She needed to sleep as Milton's ghost filled her head multiple times throughout the day and night and also the skull man that had tried to end her life. Sigh, I can't handle this anymore and I am going to quit this shit, she grabbed the water from her bedside and tried to take a sip as the glass just slipped hitting the hardwood floor and bounced coming to stop in slow motion. Her eyes closed fast as the gun shots came with feet of her. Maddison looked at her dresser where her 38 Special had been there with waiting willing to please her demands of fire power. Her mind came to her dad, he had left that one frightful night as she kissed him goodbye for the last time. Her eyes opened as she had known that she would visit the prison to meet her father's killer, Victor Cruz. She had been a little girl in court as he had cried from the sentence imposed back in 1970, he had been there in the vicinity of the crime. One eyewitness had said it was him because Victor was covered in blood as he was passed out at the scene. Tony Something had captured the man downtown, in the back of some bar. "Later today I am driving and have too" She said out loud, as it was epiphany. She grabbed the clock and set it for 9am as it would take hours to get to Florida State Prison.

Chapter 10
Victor Cruz

Florida State Prison had been very intimidating as she was on her way to meet her father's killer, 13 years prior, she had to know if he was innocent or guilty before he fried in Old Smoky. The drive had been long and about 2 hours and a half or so, coming up I-75 and 301 highways respectively. The prison had been mostly on the country-side of things. The TA had got up there in a jiffy, with still half a tank to go.

The pillars had been apart, constructed by stones of different colors. In big bold letters read Florida State Prison and she had no idea how they could live their lives in this hardened prison. Maddison had been informed Victor Cruz had been waiting for the meeting between them. She had been a bit scared as she did not know what he would say or do, but she had to find out before he died.

She dressed nicely for the occasion in her suit, jacket outfit with a nice bun that had looked almost like a professional type of a woman. She had left her 38 in the car if for some reason she had needed it, but they did not allow guns in the prison for safety reasons. Maddison had been feeling fearful and a little anxious to see the man that had supposedly killed her father, James Stranz, and ripped his neck out. Victor Cruz had been found that dreadful day in 1969, it had been clear as day as she could recall her daddy leaving for work and giving her a kiss on the cheek, "Baby, you know daddy has to work the night shift and I will be back tomorrow morning my love." James Stranz has been a very good looking man. Maddison was the spitting image of him and her mom had always been jealous of that fact. Maddison's eyes started to tear as her precious father had not made it back that next morning as he had promised. Maddison looked up above at the rainbow shining down from heaven as he had always told her that it was God's way of showing how kind he really was and to bless everyone with such a beautiful site. Maria Stranz had been a woman that had taken it hard after Maddison's father had been killed by Victor Cruz on that awful night back in 1969.

When her heart had been ripped from her body. Maria had killed herself by taking lots of pain pills and downing them with a whole bottle of vodka several years later. Maddison was sent to live in a foster home until she turned 18 years old and knew she would become a cop and finally a detective like James Stranz had been. She knew he would have been so happy.

The only two people that had been at the scene of the crime on December 23rd, 1969, had been a man that had found Victor Cruz passed out as he had the blood of the late James Stranz in his mouth from the bite wound that had taken his throat out like a lion eating his prey alive. Oh, she thought, how bad he must have felt when he passed. Tony Something had given his testimony during the trial of the People of Florida vs Victor Cruz, that he had been only 18 years old. The papers that Maddison had read had been horrible as to what he had done to her father, that he had a demonic presence that had taken over his soul for someone to rip the neck clean out. The marks from Cruz's teeth had matched to a certain extent.

Victor had been given a choice for a plea bargain from the prosecutor that had given him the choice of a life sentence or the death sentence, but Victor had pled for his life to be saved by the jury and claimed that he had been drugged. No drugs had ever been found in his body from the toxicology report. It seemed that the government had been working on something to use your DNA to actually get your blood or saliva blueprint from your person to see if it matched.

The front door had a buzzer on it. It was by appointment only on the death row wing, only a few men and women had been there. A total of ten people, including Victor Cruz. "Beep" as Maddison pushed the intercom to get one of the guards' attention. "Do you have an appointment?" The heavy accented guard had asked

Maddison through the intercom. "Oh yes, this is Detective Maddison Stranz and I am here to see Victor Cruz."

"Buzz" was the sound that had come from the door's metal lock, unlocking from the other side. No one was there to greet her. The place looked more like a hospital than a prison. The white tile floors had a brilliant shine to them and it looked like it was just waxed, the walls were fully painted in a new paint color scheme that had made it look brand new. It did not have one blemish from feet print or scuffs from other prisoners. She walked closer to the internal part of the Death wing. One skinny male with glasses that had looked like a toy cop had asked her to put any object made of metal in a basket. She had put her purse and coat jacket through the station to check for contraband. "Ma'am, do you have any weapons or knives?" "No sir and I am all clear of any weapons," she spoke to the officer. The guard with the glasses asked for her ID to see if she was on the list to get in. Maddison had flipped open her badge to show she was on the same team as the officers were. The glasses-wearing guard let her go to the next level, "Ok thanks."

Maddison made her way inside a room with a glass partition for the separation of the prisoner from the visitor. The glass was more than five, or so, inches thick. The glass had a few bullet holes from some previous inmate's mistakes. The last 13 years must have been hell for Victor she had thought.

The guards had blindfolded a man that looked to be in his late 60's as Victor had aged in the past decade. The young guard with the cop-style mustache had taken off the blindfold, his eyes had been something out of a Freddy dream where the man with knives for fingers would get you on Elm Street. His wrinkles were deep like craters as if it were a road map leading to other states in the USA. The long white beard had hung down to his chest as he was applying for the role of Santa Claus, and his weight was no more than a buck twenty.

The first words that came out of his mouth were, "Oh, Maddison, I am truly sorry for your father." She sat there cold and hard like a woman scorned from the death that never healed. She looked in his soul to see where he was at. He might have changed over the years, but he still had kind eyes. Now he had been hard-boiled by the Justice system, it did not take it easy on murderers. "I don't understand why you killed my father like some wild animal?" He had started tearing up badly like a man that is about to fry on death row would. His head shook as the white beard went from side to side. It had looked like he was not the one who had done the murder. "I know you don't believe me, but I was set up by Tony Bransford, my coworker. He had been an evil man and wanted me dead or gone because his girl had a crush on me back then. You would not believe it but I was once a very handsome man." He jetted down a small hint of smile as he remembered himself as he once was.

No, you were covered with...my father's...blood on you and Tony had found you laying there with a his throat eaten out. I remember it as clear as ever." "Tony had come up behind me as he spoke in his deep tone, telling me, 'Night night girlfriend stealer'. He had said that as he covered my mouth full of some chemical that I can still taste. I would never kill. Your father was well loved by all of us and Tony had it in for him because he had written him a ticket that day and had his car towed. He hated your father," as a sigh came over, he could not keep the tears locked away.

"I don't know why, but I do believe you and, oh my God, Tony Bransford is the father of Brody Bransford, my trainer!" Her face was a huge mess now from the revelation. "We will get this DNA fixed and I will help you, I promise before you are killed," and she meant every word of it. Victor smiled for the first time in God knows how long. "I had been trying to tell the DA and also the people on that jury that had been all white and they believed I had been the killer of your father. I was only working there and I guess I had been drugged from behind as I was fighting for my life. All I remember was...' Tears had filled his eyes again as emotions were running on high octane. "I am so sorry for your loss and I would say that we have to find Tony Bransford to get some of his DNA." His thoughts had hit her hard as she never expected for the man that took the rap, to shed some much needed light on the situation for the last 13 years. "I would have come sooner...but I had been so scared to face you and I felt like you were going to kill me, somehow." Victor put up his hand to the window, showing thanks as prisoners do to the visitors that came to visit the lonely people in prison. His blue uniform had looked like it was not washed for years as the stains had gathered on it from the many meals that Victor has had over the course of his time in prison.

Maddison had never been to a prison and all she could do was copy what Victor had done, to show respect for the framed man and she would help him no matter, unless she was killed by the monster that's been roaming the streets. "Times up!" As the guard banged on the door to get their attention from the meeting that they had been going on for, the past 30 minutes.

Victor had started yelling at the guard from inside the room. "Fuck you, pig," he shouted toward the heavy-set man that came in ready to beat him. "Victor, don't fight it," she whispered to him as he would have made it harder for him to get the DNA test that they both needed from the bite marks that had torn her father's neck apart like a wild animal had. "I will be back and please be on your best behavior so...they let me come back. I am the head detective now on a case, but I did not want to come back to the stress. It has been hell." She told him as he was being lead out from the Visitor's room. The eyes had made contact one last time, she would not see him for some time.

The rain had been coming down hard as bullets flying through the air. Her black TA had been there as it was supposed to be. As she came to the driver's side window, glass had been shattered on the seat and also the ground was blanketed. "What the hell!" she shouted and what a time to have this happen and now it was at a fucking prison to boot. Not one cop around, as she spoke to herself in a surprised way. "My gun, where...oh fuck!" The gun had been stolen as it was not next in the seat where she had left it..and a note was in the seat. ("Bitch, you are lucky but not as lucky as your dad was. I will not even use anything to knock you out. You are next.") The note had been written in some form of blood as he was warning her. She stared up into the heavens to ask her father for help. Maddison started crying as she got into the car, she knew she had a target on her back and needed to catch the killer before she was dead.

Chapter 11
The Takeover

I had been chasing Maddison as she had gone to the prison to visit Victor and I was not going to let her get away from me. She was meant to be mine and I would not let the evil take her soul to heaven yet or to his hell. She had been in the prison and I was sure she had been there for some dirt that had to be revealed. The lone standing Trans Am that had been there from the Body shop, I remembered it well, like fine wine that you swirl around to taste it, but I wanted to have her before the monster would kill Maddison and take her eyes out. That son of a bitch. It was a blood bath and the 22nd Precinct had been a killing field for us. My eyes shut remembering the horrors that follow would be in the record books. I would not be coming home again. It was a disaster.

I lay there coughing hard like I was dying, the two guards had run over to check me out in my cage of steel, like some animal that had been locked away. It was always his way and I could not control it. Nothing could control the evilness and he wanted out of me. But I was a shell and he was the ghost, together we were a killing squad. He stuck their eyes out and ripped them from the socket and they screamed as the pools of blood fell like a macabre massacre. The blood always excites him. The lawyer screamed and tried to run before we grabbed her by her hair and yanked the bitches hair out, tearing the scalp clean off leaving her brain showing. We were strong and could not be stopped. She died from the blood loss and the pain, it was like a horror movie. I could tell from my body's feeling of euphoria had erupted and gave me a hard-on from hell.

The keys had been laying on the eyeless guard's leg like a dead weight that needed removing. We got out and one of the cop cars had been left unattended. It had been a black crown Victoria with the big V8, the big daddy shotgun lay in the back like a sleeping baby and about to be awakened like a death note. My eyes were burning as I was now taking shape as a mass murder on the loose for blood, my eyes had a blood coloring to them, like some freak vampire out to suck the blood of his victims.

We drove to Maddison's apartment as I knew it by heart and wanted to see her as we had a lovely kiss last time like teenagers in love. I would not take her eyes out, but rather take her as ours, she loved us.

We waited for about 20 minutes until she was dressed in her suit and jacket. And she was not in her cop clothes and I wondered where she had been going, I might be her stalker, but who wouldn't be? She was on her way and I followed her close as she whipped across the

I-75 to her get-a-way to the prison and we waited for the right time to break in her car as the gun lay in the side seat like an easy score. Nothing was better than taking her firepower away as when we get her she would be like candy for the taking.

Whack! My hand blasted through the window shattering it all over the ground and the seat. My hand bloody as I left her a note with the monster unveiling his thoughts for her. My eyes caught the shiny revolver, it was loaded and ready to blast someone's face clean off. I looked around and no cars or guards were looking our way. She would be coming and we needed to hide out of site because she would remember my face, even thought now I looked like one of Satan's men. We would meet back at her house and try to have a lovemaking session for me and my darling Maddison and no one would stop us, as the monster would try to consume her but as myself and would fight to keep her alive. As long as I have life in me, the hell he will!

Chapter 12
I see you

Maddison had no time to make a police report, well, because they would fuck her over like some out-of-town cop that needed to keep her head out of their asses. She pushed the glass from the seat as she could still drive the mean TA. The clouds that made it look like rain was coming, the color was like a fucked-up rainbow of blacks and dark greys as they flooded the heavens. For some reason the parking lot had been empty and almost like the Twilight Zone. It was hell coming for her as the signs were not in her favor.

I wonder who broke in my car to take my gun? She thought of the people that would try this type of tactic. It was a dead end.

She had left like a roaring lightning bolt shooting through the air. The sign had read several hundred miles back to Tampa, to work on Victor's case. He had needed her and she knew that. The man did not deserve to stay in prison a day longer. "I need to help him before it's too late!" Her eyes full of tears as the water works started flowing hard and had felt like she was going to lose another good person in her life, she pounded the steering wheel as in to ask why for all the hardships she had taken in her life? Her father, her partner and of course Victor.

She looked to the East and then to west in search of how to get to get back home. She knew it, but her mind was fried and could not think to make it back home tonight. It would be best to find a nice motel, somewhere near here and also get a hot meal in her, before her strength had shut off the blood flow to her muscles. "You look like shit, Maddison Stranz!" Her hair had been frizzy to the point of no return. Some hair oil would have taken care of that but she had nothing beside the clothes that she had on her back and the suit was not going to cut it, for the night's sleep time. I will sleep naked, I don't have to impress no one. She had giggled at the thought of her man sleeping naked with her, if she had one.

Brody had been in her mind, she had kissed him and felt something wonderful. But after hearing about his father, that is beyond her reach to try to get over.

I won't be able to even workout at the fucking gym now, I have been burned and need to feel something new but how could she leave Brody Bransford. It would be hard, but if that's what the doctor called for...then so be it, she thought. The drive had been quick as she looked around for the very first place that she could catch some food. The place was Brother Joe's Diner, it had a country feel to it as the place had been constructed out of wood entirely, the wood looked like it had been there since the Great Depression. It almost seemed like a dive joint. The parking lot had been a graveyard of nothing but trash littered around like they did not know how to clean up for the folks around Gainesville.

What a shit hole, but what else can we eat besides dirt from the ground." She checked her watch as the time had gotten late, it had been almost 8 o clock on the dot. The sun was almost gone as the sky had a thunderous sound of the angels playing around the heavens, having a get together and slamming their drinks together for a wonderful time.

She walked in and saw no one in the place besides a dirty cook that had not washed his uniform in God knows how long. The man smelled like shit, Maddison had thought, better buy him some deodorant before he kills us all by his body odor. "How many you havin' dear?" The old lady behind the counter had said in a smoker's voice. She looked to be about 80 years old, she had that "I Love Lucy" vibe with the permed red hair, that had been dyed throughout the years, She smelled like old tuna that had stayed there for 2 years baking in the sun, it almost made Maddison throw up. Wow, what a crowd, I can see why they are so popular. Ok, maybe it's a mom and son who own this shit hole, meaning the cook and the server.

As Maddison had looked around at the place. it had a brilliant look to it still. The pictures on the wall had been back in the 1930s as it had looked nice at one time in its life. The tables all had this hideous cloth that smelled like vinegar-pickles with countless stains that decorated the place like a uniform. She sat down like a prisoner that was going to be served the last meal before execution.

Maddison saw the name on her uniform that had the word 'Martha'. The uniform had the 1950s appeal as they had white uniforms with red bowties that had been around the neck of the waitress. The cook just looked the like the poster boy for the happier times in America.

The menu had only one thing on it that read Southern-style pork chops in gravy. As Maddison looked up and the woman smiled with no teeth in her mouth like a Halloween pumpkin. "Is this all that you serve here?" Maddison's face uncertain why they only had one item on the menu. "Well, that's it darling and if you ain't like it you just don't know about no type of good food!" It had made her want to throw up, as the pumpkin teeth had some horrible smells coming from her gums like rotting bacon. "You going to order it or you just wastin' my time, honey? No, that will be fine Martha." The older Martha gave some kind of snicker as she took the order.

Five minutes later the food came out as it was pre-made to serve the sloppy food, Maddison knew it looked like shit, but had been starving, if you put a hot pile of dung, she was served. The food had looked like pig fat that was smeared on week-old pork. Well, it ain't going to kill me, unless it gave me food poisoning. "Can I have a water, please?" Water ain't free, it's 50 cents for it. You want it or you just wastin' my time?" "Thanks, I would like one." Old Martha scoffed like an old turtle looking to win the race against the rabbit.

After eating the old garbage, Maddison had felt bad as the food hit her hard. The bill came and it read $3.99 and an extra 50 cents for the water, that was tap water.

Maddison left the shithole and was walking past several homeless people laying on a park bench, one of them pointed at Maddison for some money, she hurried to her beat up Trans am. The same cop car that had been following her from the prison sat across the street at a Shell gas station. The windows had been blacked out and she could not tell who was in there. It all seemed wired as a stalker had been after her.

The rain started pouring down as it had looked like hell was blowing a fart of massive size. The window was getting wet and she needed to find shelter before it was going to flood the inside of the car. The traffic had looked dead as this was a little town and most likely it had been as bad as the little restaurant. She wondered if the population was the prison and the two workers at the restaurant that she had just eaten at. As she turned her head and saw the hotel, or more of a motel that she thought, it had read in big neon letters 'Vacancy' with every other letter burnt out like a some bad nightmarish place. This place gives me the creeps, she thought. The building had looked like it would not have been a motel but more or less a brothel of some sort. The color had been some sort of puke green color and the magic of it being a crack house or crack shack. The covering had been available near the front of the motel to where the car could stay dry for the night's rain.

Maddison walked feverishly toward the front door that had a bell on the front. There had been a sign that read 'Out to lunch or busy doing work if I ain't heard yous'. It was just her luck that it was a hick town. She reached up for the bell, 'ring', as the bell rang in a shrill sound that sounded like a broken bell. Wow, even the bells are more country than normal. "Who it?" The man that had written the sign had been the one character behind the voice. "Looking for a room, it said that you had rooms for rent, from the vacancy sign that was posted on the outside when I drove by." "Yeah we just one available right now" maybe he did not even graduate middle school, the way he spoke drove her crazy hearing his voice like an uneducated person. "How much is it for a night's stay?" "It be twenty," as he made snorting sounds from the amount of chewing tobacco in his mouth that had sounded like wet sloppy wetness.

The room was something out of Africa, it made Maddison feel like throwing up after having the Southern pork with nothing but animal fat. Animal heads surrounded the desk at the front of this small hotel. The man had been something out of Africa too; to be blunt. He had a patch over his right eye. His leg had been a wooden peg. I wonder if he had been eaten by one of the animals from the wall, Maddison thought. He was tall and could have been six feet tall. The body odor had put a tight grip on her stomach as the whole scenario had been terrifying. The room is still open if's you want it? His eye had been looking away from Maddison as he talked. It confused her if he knew she was a woman by his eye sight. He sat down at what was a wooden desk with a cherry wood finish. A sign had read Jason Parker in bold italics. Maddison looked around at the animals, she had seen a lion, a tiger and a bear oh my. Something out of the Wizard of Oz.

"Twenty dollars it be for the night, Miss." Maybe it was better to sleep in the car she thought and at least the animal could not get her in there, but it felt like Noah's Ark was going to sail in front of the small motel. The rain belted down with full force, splashing the window with its hard drops. The Trans Am would need to have the carpets cleaned from all this rain.

Maddison turned back as she passed him the $20 that had been her last cash. She needed to get to an ATM or use the credit card that had been a back up, she didn't like to use because the interest rates 28 percent which would take a long time to pay off.

Jason Parker had lead the way to show her, the room that he had saved for her had been 609 which made no sense, because it only had one floor which had a few rooms connected like a duplex. Twenty bucks for this shithole and I could have found a much nicer one if the rain had not been pissing down so hard. "Oh...I wanted to let you know that we do have a VHS player with a few tapes that you can watch if you like. The ice is down the hall and here is your room key." His teeth had been pretty rotten and it felt like he had never brushed them or at least it made Maddison wonder if he had someone to kiss.

The room was clean, but it had smelled like partially decaying bodies that had been buried under the bed. Maddison had the curiosity, to check for the smell. Her eyes moved as she looked around from where she had been looking from under the bed. The front window had been able to see through it, but her eyes caught the police cruiser that had been in the two other places. It was like something bad was about to happen like some low budget horror that had been an omen for her death. The rain had been coming down, the car could not been seen from Maddison's vision, she felt her hair stand on end as it might have been that jerk that stole my 38 Special?" The night would be cold and spooky like something out of a mystery. She felt her legs start to buckle as her head was spinning like something had hit her hard. She did not know but maybe the food had been laced with something sinister she thought. That old bitch must have slipped me something. Her eyes saw something that looked like Brody as she passed out.

Chapter 13
I am home, Baby

Her eyes were shaky as one eye opened but her vision was something strange as if a mirage had been in front of her face. She had no recollection of how or why Brody stood in front of her like something scary but pleasurable. Maddison did not know if it was a dream or actually reality at its finest. "Hi Maddison, you had let me in last night." "To be honest I had to drive up here from Tampa after you called me." "It can't be possible Brody, I don't remember anything about it." Maddison's heart started humming a beat faster and faster.

Her heart told her she wanted him like fine diamonds that sparkled a thousand times shinier than the most precious stone in the world.

They sat there in the bed naked as she had given herself to Brody with pleasure. Brody had her in his grasp and it was more than the tough Maddison Stranz could ever imagine.

Something was magical as she had not given herself since Jonathon had been hers in the past.

Maddison looked down and her body was naked and it was something that she could not think of. "Tony, did we have sex last night?" "It was better than I could ever imagine, Maddison. You are a sexy woman. I have these feelings for you and you for me." Brody had looked at her as he touched her arm with kindness and passion. He reached over with a kiss to her lips as it was love that she felt. Stunning magic had transpired in this room. Maddison did not flinch, she could not resist this man that had something on her. It was not something she could understand, but to keep going with it. She had felt so sadden by her partners death and had been at the mercy of depression.

Brody grabbed her with his powerful arms as she was his now. The power struck her with love that was breathtaking. Brody caressed her supple breast with tenderness. His mind had been in a different world with her. For some reason the monster did not try to take her life now, but it would come about in the future.

Maddison kissed him with slow passionate kisses that ravished her body making her moist and feeling turned on. His member entered her with authority as she cried out with pleasure. It had been heavenly for her as she had reach a climax at the same time he had finished inside her with glory. Sighs came over them as she rolled into him with affection and cuddles that filled his heart with love for once in his life.

Maddison looked deep in his eyes as something had been strange for the way he stared at her with a kind of red tint to his glossy eyes. She wondered if it was the lovemaking or just the red color of this handsome man that had ravished her body. The feeling had been more than what she could have asked for.

But how did he get her and why can't I remember what had happed. "Brody, this might be forward, but in my line of work...I don't get the chance to meet someone who I can connect with like you. I felt my heart tell me I loved you from the beginning, Brody." Her heart was his now and she had the time now to spend with a man that she could call her own. "Maddison, it was also me that had found you to be breathtaking and my heart told me that you were mine." Maddison had woken up to find her bed empty with no one in sight. I must be losing my mind, did I not just have fucking sex with Brody? She had reached down and felt her vagina with her fingers to see if it had been penetrated by him. Her findings were unsure as nothing had felt different. Her thoughts were, well, I should have felt something in there, but after all...I am a virgin, she cracked a smile. The whole scenario had been something like a dream for Maddison. She had to get back to find him and see if he was real this morning or had he been just a dream that was amazing with love and affection that a woman needed by her man. Time would tell is it was just a dream. Her mind was set. Brody would be stalked, " Hope you don't mind a stalker, Brody!"

She had lost her mind as she raised both of her hands in the air as if to call for something to happen and to get her life going in the right way. It was time to get out of here and get back home. She would sleep for just a little longer and get her ass on the move when the rain stopped. Her window would be broken still and she would need to visit the Pontiac dealer, where she had bought her black beauty. She looked over at her bedside clock, it read 7am on the dot. The Bible was on the end table, too. She grabbed it with her hand as it was meant to be seen. The first words were, "Thou shalt repent for thy sins", if Maddison had sex with him she would repent to God as he was her lifeline after her father's death. I will go back to church and I know that I have sinned in my mind. But God would show her the way. She smiled as her luck would change for the worst. Life would be hell for her coming up. Nothing could have gotten her ready for what was to come. She closed her eyes tight and when she got some answers, then the puzzle would fit in all the right places. She saw her father as she was about to dream.

And the memories had been good to put her to sleep.

Chapter 14
The escape

The motel had been my enemy and also my closeness to Maddison. She had made love with me in a blink of an eye, I left before the monster came or he would have eaten her alive. I knew better, to get my ass out of there before it was too late.

The man at the front desk had deserved what he had gotten, the bloodshed had been like fountains of blood flowing wild from the massacre. The monster needed blood as I had taken another life. The count had been more than six now, but who is keeping track of it. The motel manager on staff had given me one hell of a problem as he tried to stop me, but I had killed him with my hammer, smashing his brains out like hamburger meat scattered all over his desk. The cops were on my trail and I had no chance to keep this up before my ultimate arrest. At least I got to be with Maddison for one last time. The animal heads had been wild as he had hunted them with little remorse. Nothing worse than a hunter. The lion head had been a mighty kill for anyone.

I was now a wanted man on the loose and if they caught me, well, I would be on death row. His eyes had been taken so he could not see my soul. I could see cops were waiting and ready to take me in, I had to get away. The building next to the motel was a gun store and I needed a gun so I would fight to the death. I would not go to prison and if I did, it would have been a mental institution for the criminally insane.

"Hey! Where are you going?" The mustache cop had noticed me as I was a sore thumb sticking out with blood caked on my clothes. He pulled his gun at me, his eyes narrowed and was ready to fire on me if I took one more step. I paused in mid-stride as I was leaving the motel, I raised my arms above my head as he had me with his 38 revolver pointed at me. The cop rushed over as he kicked me to floor. "You're under arrest for the murders of several people including the clerk that you killed in cold blood. I am Detective Lee Stevens with the Gainesville Police Department." He was not like a detective but a plain-clothes police officer with the blue uniform to match. Lee had been following me like a bloodhound, there was a manhunt all around the state of Florida.

"Where's your ID?" Officer Stevens had been tracking me since I had come to Gainesville. I gave him the ID, he would have to take me in. I had no way to get away from this situation. The monster had hidden away deep and in his world, waiting. "Brody Bransford, you under arrest." Officer Stevens pulled out a little laminated card, "You have the right to remain silent. If you give up that right, anything you say can and will be used against you in the court of law. You have the right to an attorney. If you cannot afford one, one will be appointed to you as your public defender. Do you understand these rights as I have read them to you?" "Yeah," I said. "Why did you kill those people?" He looked shocked as if he saw a monster standing in his presence like a fable. He grabbed me off the ground. The officer pushed me in is car like a rag doll being thrown into the trash. I shook my head in disgust. My life would never be the same again. I would have been wonderful to see love for the first time with Madison as we made love. I never wanted to hurt her, but at least the monster could not get her anymore.

The cop car had been a traditional black and white. He had the station on as many cops were taking over the radio. I looked out the window to where I could see Maddison had been. Now, I had now way to escape as the cage had me like a trapped dog waiting to get out. We drove away and the next stop: jail.

Chapter 15
On my way home

The birds were chirping and Maddison woke up from the sounds of Mother Nature, letting her know that it was time to wake up. Boom, the sound echoed in the room from someone pounding, Maddison thought what the hell just happened. "Hello, who are you looking for?" Her eyes fluttered in the anticipation of what they would say. "Gainesville Police. There was a murder this morning!" His voice had been yelling through the door. "Open up, we need to check the rooms, to make sure everything is ok." She wondered if it was a real cop or the stalker that had been chasing her from the prison. He had been dressed as cops did. His badge had read Lopez on his shiny badge. "What the hell is going on? I could have been killed!" She opened the door with just the chain bolted and she saw his eyes had been kind, she thought he would not let her get hurt or killed. "I am a cop, too. I am lead detective on the monster case in Tampa," she said with positive attitude. "Ma'am, we might have the killer in custody, we would need you to come down and see if you recognize this person of interest." Maddison's face was a blur as everything did not seem real to a certain affect.

Brody had been there and she knew it, he fucked me and left me, how could he? Her tears started flowing as a massive flood had just sank the world. Her eyes closed with a flick of them. She felt the burn as her sleep had not been there. "Officer Lopez, why did you come to my room?" It was funny that he had picked her room because, well, no one else had been staying in this shit hole. First, Brother Joe's had poisoned her with that disgusting food that they had thought it was something to die for or maybe I would die she thought, as emotions had run miles in her mind.

"Miss...we were told by your husband that you and him had been on your honeymoon, is that right?" "What fucking person are you talking about, sir?" "So you don't know a Brody Bransford?" The cop said with a curious look on his face, his brow was creased. Maddison defending herself from the man that stood in front of her asking the serious questions.

Maddison looked up as she had gazed at the ceiling trying to get away from the ruthless questions that had been thrown her way. She must have been the crazy one for hearing this cop tell her that Brody had been her husband. "I need you to come down to the station and please verify the information." The cop had been very serious as was Maddison when she was taking perps in her precinct. Her mentor had been taken away by the evil skull man that had robbed the family diner.

Maddison looked down at her attire, her shaker had been fine, but the panties had been there with no shorts to match. Her eyes opened as the embarrassment had been too much. "Be right back." She covered her front and backside. She closed the door that had 601 on it. No wonder the cop tried not to let her go, she smiled as she got into her clothes wearing a shirt that read Rock Star. She put on her acid-washed jeans with a pair of white Nikes. She grabbed the handle of the door and before her eyes was Lopez standing there waiting for her like a patient cop would have. "Let me ask you, officer, are you a detective working the monster case on your own?" She asked with a concerned look on her face. "He will be booked on the charges and face the Old Smoky as he will be fried. He will be heading over to the FBI and the boys over there will eat him alive. They have lie detector test for serious criminals." Maddison would go and see him and ask why did you leave her? She might be seeing him as a burnt lobster frying in his pot of hell. The sounds of the popping would be like some sort of steak frying and burning until he was nothing more than steak was coming up and letting you know that dinner was ready. The thought of something atrocious was making her sick to her stomach. I love him I thought. Did he come over and fuck me in my dreams or reality? The detective had stood there lighting his cigarette and as he took out his trusty Zippo lighter with ease and a flick of the wrist, the fire hit the end of the white cigarette that was some sort of a rolled-up cigaerette. Wow, that stinks like hell, Maddison thought. "Are you ready? We need to head over to the FBI building where his cell would be. It's in Downtown Tampa off of Franklyn Street. You can ride with me?" It seemed like he had been interested in her and he was not a bad looking man, but rather a fat man at about 300 pounds. He sure as hell liked doughnuts she thought. "No, I will drive my car. Let's keep it causal, Detective Lopez." He smiled like a fat boy likes his cake and ice cream. His mind must be thinking about getting to lunch, Maddison thought, with a small smile that popped out like a sore thumb. "Are you ok, ma'am?" he said. Maddison gave him the A-Ok sign on her hands. Because, well, life just got much harder than she would ever know. The chubby cop lead the way.

Chapter 16
The FBI

I had been lead away in the way I felt was a horror mystery in the perfect sense, I had never killed anyone but would they believe me or not? Well, after the 6 or so bodies that the monster had ripped apart, they would give me the electric chair and send me to hell. That fucking game had possessed me like I was some insane killer on the loose from some institutional housing like I really belonged there, but I did not do anything wrong

As we pulled up, my chauffeur had taken me in cuffs. The place had been built to keep criminals at bay, it looked like I might get killed by one of the big boys. "Shut up, are you talking to your self or what?" He had caught me in the midst of talking out loud. The funny part is I had been acting crazy now and sure enough, they will write a report on me and tell the jury that I am a crazy as a shithouse rat as my grandmother from Italy used to say. God rest her soul.

The facade of the massive structure looked like a mini Empire State Building. The Agent that had me looked a bit intimidating in the worst way. He was a massive man standing over 7 feet tall. He made me look tiny. His black suit was crisp like he had spent hours ironing his clothes, the shoes looked like a real type of a pro did it, he thought, because of the shine to them, he must be a prick. "I need you to follow my lead or you will have trouble. I don't think you want this type of trouble", Agent Terry Lee said. "This is a real holding facility, not that cake walk where you killed three people in cold blood. One of the cops was my brother," the man said in a stern voice. "I don't know what your MO is?" His face had been upset and I felt I was his punching bag. His green eyes bore into me like fire and brimstone. The building was a big three story and the bars clashed on the outside. They really did not want anyone to get out of Fort Knox. The FBI agent Lee had been ready to give me to the dogs for their feeding time. I never thought we would have gotten caught, but even the best of them have to take what's coming to them, I will never give them an easy case, as I smiled at him with my red eyes. My eyes glowed bright red with fury as I was ready to kill this fucking wimp. The interior had been more like a crazy house for a lot of the places that I had read about in many of my horror books.

My hands had been cuffed rather tight as they had no mercy for a guy like me. "The Monster" is what all the papers called me before my capture, 1982 had the death of my soul, Satan had taken me from God and cursed me to a life of killing.

"Sit over here, at this table. I want to get your attention fast and quick before I beat the shit out of you so fast your head would spin!" He had been the real giant, I thought with some laughter to boot. He stood over me and ready to kill me if I spoke out of line. One of the men I had killed had been his brother and that's what he had claimed to me in his rage. My eyes closed as his sour breath was gagging me, he could have at least brushed his teeth, I thought with a mild thought.

"What you did was a fucking…shit, I lost my words. You are a low life piece of trash! You are plain evil and you will see the electric chair if it's the last thing I do!" He was now back in seat, the tape player has been playing, even though he's not telling me about the recordings.

He's trying to get me with entrapment. The world had been spinning and I thought that I might have lost my lunch. "I did nothing wrong, Jack!" The man looked at me with such fury and intensity, his head had steam coming off like a hot dog after you took the wiener out of the boiling pot of water. He came closer as his lips were only a few inches from my face. His mouth puckered up in a form that he would use to try to demoralize me in a way that no one would ever think to do. I was much bigger in muscles and with the inner power of the monster, well, this prick would have no chance to get away with that on the street. I would have cut his tongue out and feed it to him in little bit-size portions, he would swallow every piece with love and happiness.

As his spittle hit my face, the particles had fallen in my mouth like some sweat that had dropped in for a visit. My eyes clenched until I saw the black dots that you see. But mine was his face slashed and torn off the bone.

"Ahhhh!" He screamed as I bit his nose off with the coppery taste that filled my taste buds. The beast had come to play and the blood splatter was like a life-size puddle of goo and meat. He grabbed what was left of his nose. "Help!" His goons rushed in with their billy clubs smashing my brains in as I passed out from the damage.

Chapter 17
My waking

My mind was black as my dreams were filled with the past events that had shaped my world. I could see my fathers face as I stabbed him to death and it made me sad. I had not known I was a killer, but had the inner working of a mass murderer like Bundy. The poor woman that I had killed and for what? Who knew it but the monster always had his way. The mind was funny as it was controllable from another person or evil entity.

The banging had been loud as my eyes opened from the pain that flowed through my body. Nothing had ever hurt so badly physically. My strength was good but pain had been the same, so I was part human and could easily be killed if hurt bad enough.

"Fuck you, pig!" One of the men shouted in the background which made me cringe because I was at Federal detention facility that had housed many of killers from the past 70's and 80's, I would be next in line for my chance to die in the waiting game of death row. I could not think of the years of waiting for the appeals to go and go until I was waiting for the governor's last stay. He did not save me from my hell that awaited me like a knife slowly going through my heart killing me slower than a snail crossing a mile stretch of land.

"Time for count!" The voice called in a deep tone that sounded like a man that did not take shit from prisoners. The bars had been that off white painted look with nothing to look at through the bars. The floor had been painted with white lines that ran down the walk. It had a feel like it was military boot camp. I laid in my bed as I could not muster myself to get up, they must have hit something in my brain to make the wiring go limp. I closed my eyes as the lights were dimming. "Get your ass up shit head!" The guard spoke in a nasty tone. He had been pissed that another jail bird piece of shit had not followed directions. He looked through the bars pointing his finger at me with a 'get up or I am coming for you' stare. "I don't feel good, your boys beat the piss out of me! So fuck off, sucker!" The bald black man was no joke around the FBI facility, he had been known to kill some of the past prisoners.

His nickname had been Big Thunder as his size was well over several hundred pounds. His eyes had a glossed over look to them as if he had gotten his high before coming to his job to torture his men in the cells. "I am going to count to the count of three, punk, or else I am going to kick your ass and stick this size 14 up your ass so far that you will be making size 14 shoes all day long and you dig, boy?" I had no choice but to get up or the cops would end me before I ever made it to court. Not much I could do against anyone. The monster had pushed me inside to start something with officer Big Thunder, which he had tattooed on his arm that had an earthquake under the words. His double-chin giggled ferociously with the jelly jiggles. "Now, since you got up, repeat your number!" "Prisoner Number 23, Brody Bransford."

He had flicked his tongue as if he was tasting some sort of pie it had seemed. No wonder he had gotten so big. He left to his next cell who was asked their number and they replied with ease.

It had been sometime and as the day progressed without hearing from a public defender or being able to get my one phone call in. I had figured I would ask Big Thunder to see if he was in the mood to let me get it in. I had money on my phone card that I had purchased from the jail store, if you had money, then you could live your life somewhat better than the poor motherfuckers that had looked for crumbs from the other prisoners.

"Hey, come here!" I shouted from the distance and his head turned as if he heard it was dinner time. "What you want now?" "I need to make my one call please." I looked like shit and felt like I had been run over, to tell you the truth. My head throbbed as the pounding never subsided. His eyes were more kind, when you asked nicely, well, then they might treat you better. Who knows when I might be able to leave this hell hole crazy house, that was my nick name for this insane mad house. I could not even get out of room because I had ripped the guys nose clean off like a piece of beef jerky, being a cannibal might not be so bad. As he came back with a rotary phone from the 1920's, "Look, you got 5 minutes to get your call done or I am pulling the plug on your little conversation if you ain't done in time, I gots to be very hard on all of yous before you all try to take advantage of us nice people," he said in a type of country accent. As I dialed the 8 digit number for my old girlfriend, I had no idea if she would pick up or not, hell maybe she moved her location. I had loved Martha and I was a fool at the time, at least the monster did not have me by my balls. I loved Maddison and she had no idea why I left. My insides were almost going to rage and it had been a smart move for her before it was too late for her. Being with Madison and ejaculating inside her might actually have put my seed inside her. Ring, ring the sound of the phone had not yielded an answer yet. The voice answered on the line and it had been her voice. "It's Brody, I am in trouble Martha. Could you come over here and come see me?" She was silent like a mouse, the only sound had been her breathing. "Oh Brody, God has put you back in my life for good, oh how I have thought of you for the last 4 years. Oh course darling, I will be right over." Her voice had been friendly unlike the guards that controlled this nut house. "I am at the FBI center for holding, I will explain when you get here." "Baby, I am on way, it will take me some time to get over there, but I am so very happy to see you!"

The phone went dead from Big Thunder shutting the phone off in a quick grip of the button. "Hey, I was still talking to her!" His big ass will be dead before I leave this place and it will be a thrill kill for us. I smiled as I thought how fun it would be to cut his legs off and make him eat them while I smiled and toasted a glass of wine in his honor.

The night had been unbearable for the first night in my own worst nightmare. I had hoped that Martha would help me get of here and I would just play coy with here and make her think nothing more than marrying and having a baby. I would lie and deny all of the charges that had been put over my head like some failed attempt to hold me hostage in a miserable life to live in this shit hole. Nothing was worse than prison itself. My eyes were burning, someone had to die soon or I would have no control over who he killed next.

My cell was a concert cell with the traditional bars that were made of steel, one toilet and sink and, of course, no place to masturbate. Sex always made me feel nothing so no deal breaker on that, but Maddison had been different, she was my soul mate. We would be lovers and she had my seed now, planted in her it at that motel where we fucked like rabbits in heat. Her smell, I could still breath it in and taste her with lust.

Breakfast call came at a quarter to 7am and the menu was cereal and cakes in the morning and a sad sack of shit for the milk in a bag, That's what the federal system had to offer. Only if I could break out.

"Wake your asses up or I am going to have to put my size 14 in your ass!" Big Thunder was going to die or I am not worth living. He would bite the seat before I left this shit hole. He was like the black dictator in this housing unit so be it while you have the power for now I thought dreamy thoughts in my sick mind.

He stopped in front of my cage staring at me, "That hell got into your eyes, boy, They look red or some form of hate coming to me?" He was toying with me or trying to make the monster come to life sooner than later. You got a visitor coming, but you need to see that shrink before your visitor can see your ugly mug. Hahaha," his laugh came on like some hard ass trying to be funny.

I stood up and held my ground and I was not going to let him tease me. "Be ready in 5 minutes or you are going like that, and make sure you brush your teeth before you kill us of stank breath."

Five minutes had arrived faster than I had wanted, I could see that he had a billy club waiting for me if I was out of line, He would get his unexpectedly sooner than later. My smile had turned into a joker laugh, all I needed was a purple hat and some fucked up face paint for two sickos. It did not bother me to kill, It felt like when you exercise at the gym and this my ability to do the work of the monster, If the people did not like it, I did not care what anyone thought about my monster IOU's for everyone. Who knows maybe they found daddy? Big Thunder crossed his arms as he was by waiting for some lip, well, to knock me to the moon and back. I knew I had to get this low life under my feet. I had felt like he was pushing his luck with Joe Buddy or whoever was in his way, but a man like me would guard his weakness against attackers. "You takes more time than a woman, boy," he rushed at me with the quickness of a Pro Bowl NFL lineman coming for that quarterback. He cuffed me as I had no choice, I could have killed him if I would have grabbed him by his fat neck and strangled the life out of him. I had to play it cool and take the insane charge to my grave and live my life in prison most likely or if I could break out of this joint like something out of the movie. I could have the girls come help me escape like the movie "One Flew Over the Cuckoo's Nest", except I would not be killed by the Chief. A smile came over me because maybe I had hope after all in this horrid life. Martha would be here for me and hopefully Maddison would come later to break me out of this hell-hole.

"At least you're not that dumb or else I would have knocked you out." His eyes stared holes in me as if he was going to eat me.

The shrink's office has been near the front door, Mental Health Specialist Dr. Brian Mann, His plaque had been in gold letters on a plain black door. It was funny how his office had been the rare one and not had the white door and the silver lettering. I tilted my head as I would never understand human nature to show off. Big Thunder pushed me in with full force, my knees slide into first base. "Ouch!" I called out in spite of him throwing me in the place like some piece of garbage. "Well, hello there, you must be Brody Bransford?" The doctor looked at me as he spoke in such a nice tone, that you would have felt right at home.

The desk had picture of him and his family, such a nice family, "Well, as long as you're a doctor, then you can make your own diagnosis of me. I have someone inside that is controlling me." The doctor just stared at a crazy person, he shook his head trying to figure out if the crazy talk was going for the home-run hit directly out of the park.

The doctor was older and maybe I could have guessed in his late 50's. His head was bald as a bowling ball and his shape was rather overweight for a man of his age. When you lived in America, then you would get fat when you worked behind a desk. The clock rang, 7:30 on the dot as the bells rang out. The doctor smiled at me with an attempt to get my trust.

Please have a seat as he pointed to the empty chair that stood in the middle of the room. I was not sure if he was going to give me a treat for being such a good boy. "I have read about your case and I would like to run a battery of tests to see what your diagnosis would be for a court of law." I was not scared, I felt like I was in good hands.

"Is that your family?" His eyes squinted at the picture. "Why, yes, that's my wife and boy, thanks for your support as my patient." He smiled as he gave his statement, "What ever you talk about is between us."

The feeling had been horrible as this man had been pushing me to tell my story to him as he thought he was a God of some sort. He pulled his pad and pen out as he was going to take my life's story and turn it into something that he could control and use it against me in a court of law. He was not on my side and more or less an evil person pretending to be someone decent. Shit, who in the hell would be good in this place. If he was anything like Big Thunder, well, I might as well get sent to hell faster in a body bag sent to the incinerator. "Doc...can I call you that?" You can call me whatever you want, but don't call me late for dinner." He chuckled. Ok, now we have a funny guy, that's his tactic and I can also give him some of the medicine that can make him think that I have a brain. "What are we having for dinner?" He looked at me with an expression that said it all. He thought I was normal and would be sent to the prison faster than Speedy Gonzalez.

"Well, if you must know I am a kind man and never hurt anyone and that's that. If you don't believe me then just give me a lie detector test!" I shouted at him as I did not give a fuck.

One way or another I would have to escape or he would send me to the chair laughing. Fucking shrinks never cared anyway. "You know what...we have a new way to help you get over your mental problems...We have hydrotherapy in a nice burning pot of water that will make you come to your senses, Mr. Bransford." The doctors eyes moved side to side like some sort of cocaine addict in a meltdown for not getting his local fix. He turned to his desk and opened one of the locks and I heard the sound make a key-turning noise. He looked into it with passion and knew he had the upper hand and loved every minute of it. I could see the book with a cross on it and I knew the Bible talk was about to come into play. I know the Devil had my nuts in a vise grip that was tearing them little by little. "Doctor, I am not taking that book and you can shove it where the sun don't shine." I was being frank as I could, I could have said stick it up your ass. He shook his head as he was pissed and I had ruined his speech that he was about to throw my way in terms of religious talk. The chair had been giving me pain as much as Dr. Al Lenok. He sighed with a great big breath of stinky air that smelled like stale cigarettes and coffee. We could have been friends, I thought while I would have ripped your eyes out and kept them as a trophy along with the others. I knew that they would be looking for the eyes of the monster's victims that I had stored in the backyard. It had been a place that they could never find. We had a bunker that Tony, my father, had made back when World War 2 had ended. Only I knew of this bunker and no one else could find it.

The doctor hit a button as the small light flickered and flashed. The big motherfucker came back and the last thing I saw was his club knocking me out.

Chapter 18
Love spell

Maddison had been upset as she drove to the FBI station to confess to Brody Bransford, her love. She needed him more than anything in this world. He had put a spell on her after they had made beautiful love together. It almost felt like some type of Cupid had struck her ass with an arrow out of nowhere.

The drive had been quick as the officer had led the way in his black and white. The FBI headquarters in Tampa had been something that was over her pay grade as a detective in the 22nd Precinct. She had been saving up and a few weeks ago when Maddison had gotten her shield for detective, well, she had said fuck it and went out to the mall and bought one of the most expensive Gucci suits, purse and shoes that had been there. It was a gorgeous Navy color that made her green eyes shine even more to offset the blue color and the elegance of Gucci. "I hope I can help him get out of here and come home to Mama. I missed my man." Her face was full of smiles as she knew she had become his soul mate and needed her man.

Shit, she never thought that she would be in love with a killer like Bundy or some other sicko, but he would never hurt her.

As she came back to reality, the chubby officer tapped the glass to let her know that she had arrived and needed to follow him to the intake station and to discuss the case to try to put him away for good. She would never hurt him and would protect him as she would not let the awful cops hurt him with their words or beating him and throwing away the key.

They walked in, the place had a picture of the President Ronald Reagan standing next to his wife smiling, someone had scribbled on the picture with the words 'greatest president' with a heart next to him. Maddison had not been a fan of either party, but she had enjoyed how Reagan had changed the drug game, seized most if not all of Columbia's cocaine distribution in the United States of America.

Officer Lopez had introduced her to a man that was a dapper don of a man and if Maddison had been a single woman, well then she would have dated him with open arms. He was a man of darker complexion that looked like he was full Italian. His face was young for a man with grey hair and a defined face that could represent sexy for a woman. His hair was combed back perfectly, his green eyes were gorgeous to the point of her not being able to look away. "Yes, this is Agent Stone and he will be taking over from now on for this case." "Well Miss Stranz, I have heard amazing things about you back home, you are the so called Rookie of the Year." The chubby cop had left with a quick introduction for these two to meet. "He means well, darling." Maddison did not like being called darling by random men that looked down on her as a woman. "Could you just keep it Miss Stranz, Agent Stone?" He nodded at the statement made by a woman that was all of everything that agent Stone ever wanted in a woman.

He did a flick of the arm, sent her into the room that had been as bare as a whistle except a couple of bolted down chairs. A glass of water as they always had water for the scared person being interviewed about anything in a police station or the FBI that would sure be much more of a challenge.

"Have a seat Miss Stranz, I would like to go over some things that have been bothering me for the longest time as you may well know since you have also been on this case. Well, damn! Can you tell me why you are sleeping with Mr. Bransford, the accused killer and by all standards, it seems like you have gotten caught with your hands in the cookie jar."

He seemed furious as his eyes were more like a small tear looking into her being. It made her feel like saying, 'well, it's none of your business and if I want to love this so called monster, well, so be it'. But how do I even know I had sex with him, it was a fucked-up dream if that did not happen. The agent snapped his fingers serial times as he tried to wake Maddison out of her day dream. Maddison shook her head as she was trying to regain her mind to focus on the task at hand. "Sorry, I am not feeling right and I need to lay down. My stomach is making me feel so bad and I might need throw up before I pass out. The Agent arose and headed for Maddison to get her before something happened on his watch. "Put your head down till we can get you someplace to lay your head down and catch some rest."

The room had been for people that did not have stomach to keep going and to get some rest so they could be given some time to clear their head and come back to the interview. The room had been plain and the bed had that paper on it like she got to lay on in every doctor's office that she had ever been. It almost felt like it had been prison or a form of that. She sat up and there had been a bucket that Agent Stone had left for her.

I can't believe it but it feels like morning sickness, her stomach had been getting bigger and it had been only what seemed like a day ago. But she would need a test to see if it was true or just nerves piling up.

Brody was close as she could really sense that he was near and felt like they were more of a single person. The part that was strange had been the fact, that she had not even cared for him prior to the so called sex dream or was it reality?

They had returned Maddison back to interrogation room that had felt scary and being locked up in that room had made her feel even more lonely than she was already feeling. "Now, have a seat. Are you going to talk or would you like an attorney?" She closed her eyes remembering her time with her man, no, he was her everything in this world. He was the only person to show love since her father had been killed. Her heart beat faster that it was him that got her here in the first place. What if he is a killer and girl, could you still love him like you already do? "I love him!" Maddison had shouted out during the recording session. "I am truly sorry that I said that. My mind is not in the place that I need it to get to. I am going to decline to speak to you." She had put her foot down with authority.

He came close and whispered in her ear..."You will be staying here now too, until we get some answers from you and Brody." She knew that she could not talk or end up in this case for both of them to go to Old Smoky.

Chapter 19
Hard times

Maddison sat there in her cell with one other woman that had been sleeping like sleeping beauty the whole time she had been locked away. The cell had a woman's touch with a poster on the wall of Al Pacino and Robert De Niro from a scene of each in their respective roles from Scarface and Taxi Driver. Love really makes you do stupid things she thought while sitting up and wishing she had the will power to not be in Brody's grasp. The closer she was the more her mind took a beating and wished for her to be his forever.

At the gym he had kissed her after their session of working out and it had little feeling but just a kiss really. If she could get a call out to McDonald, her captain, well, maybe he could send someone or pull strings to get her home and away from the federal system.

"Stranz, are you ready to answer my questions so you can go home quicker?" Agent Stone spoke to Maddison in a condescending tone. Maddison got up and walked over the bars to talk to him. "I don't know anything, Agent Stone. You can't keep me here against my free will!" Maddison was at a loss for words and needed to talk before they made her go insane. "I love him is all I can say, Agent Stone, and I don't believe he would ever hurt anyone. I mean that on my word as a detective!" Agent Stone had a face that was hard to see through to know if he was going to believe you or through the book at you, as she compared the FBI to the city police working in the 22nd Precinct as a rookie detective.

"Your so-called lover is booked on killing three people at your Precinct's jail and you still hold him in your heart as a fucking Christian! Wake up and smell the coffee. You must be drunk in love or just as nuts as he is!" His face was beet red, he knew she was a damn fool for prancing around like an idiot saying how much she had loved this sick person. They were going to fry her lover in a chair where most, if not all, the bad people went when they were doing Murder One for God's sake. Maddison grabbed the bars and tried to break them apart, she spat in his face with a mouth full of saliva.

The agent wiped it away as if he was not fazed by this lovesick woman. It was going to be a long road ahead for Maddison Stranz and she was possessed by the evil entity that had taken over her body after sex with the monster. It was like she was the pupil and he was the master, making her out to be crazy. That was his plan and to give life to his child that would inherit the monster next after Brody Bransford was executed on Florida's death row. She would be sent along with him for accessory to the murders if she did not face the music and turn on him before it was too late.

The smile came out big and wide for the Agent Stone. He had both of them in his grasp and would make her pay for spitting in his face as well and take away her shield for good. She would be a convicted murderer and do as he pleased, well because he could do anything in this field as an agent with the FBI. "Maddison, we will give you a lie detector and see how we do? If you did not help your so-called lover kill these people then we don't have a problem, but I am charging you with assault on me, you...BITCH!!!" He screamed as the spittle flew all over her face like acid rain coming from hell.

Maddison knew she was in trouble for herself and also for Victor Cruz, the innocent man on death row. How could she love a man whose father was killed by her father? That was the power of the evil spirit roaming in Brody's body. In the worst case, she would end up in the woman's wing with her lover in the Florida State prison. "I will be back in 15 minutes to bring you to the lie detector room to determine your honesty in these murders. If you want a lawyer, now is the time to lawyer up, Miss Stranz?" Maddison knew this was the end of her before she knew it.

The lie detector

The room became a way for her and she knew that many days and nights to come would be here. She could not turn on the love of her life. Brody Bransford was her man, her everything, indeed. She could hear the women screaming for help as they were all criminals anyway.

"Maddison,...are you ready for the test?" "Go fuck yourself, Stonehenge!" The two woman guards were there and at his command, waiting to punish Maddison. They were two beefy woman and if you saw them on the street and you could say they look like men. "Bring her ass to me!" Agent Stone pointed at Maddison with such evil eyes, that the devil would have been scared.

Maddison went towards the bed, she knew they were going to come for her. She got into her stance with a 'come here, ladies' taunt, see what this sexy blonde has for you. They were on either side of her and they looked for the sign for when they could pounce on the single prisoner in the corner. The woman on the left with the big gut made her pounce like a bear going for the kill. Maddison was ready and had her hand in the kill position and ready for her attacker. Her palm hit the overweight bodybuilder directly in the nose with such force, the bone fragment was sticking out like a broken chicken wing at KFC. The guard fell with a crash as if her soul was being taken out. The blood splatter hit Maddison on her face. The other guard pulled out her billy club and smashed the hell out of Maddison with such force she almost lost her life with the power of the guard's blows. The last thing Maddison saw was the face of Brody and his kiss as she went unconscious.

The hospital

The bright lights shone down on her like she was in heaven. She saw her father give her a kiss before he left that night. (I will be back before you know it.). The dream had been real as if he was there. She could feel the tears stream down her cheeks. The Devil came to her with the smell of dead animals and the smell was unreal. The face had been black with fire glowing in the eyes.

"Come with me!" She had turned her head fast as she could to get away from him before he took her soul away.

The face she saw was Agent Stone, "Miss Stranz, I think we can now call you a murderer. You just killed one of our guards here at this facility. We are locking you for good on one count of murder, I will make sure you never get out again." "I was protecting my baby." She closed her eyes as she said those dreadful words that she had now felt in her body. How could she know she had his baby in her womb? She knew it.

"Let's get some pee in here for the test, Maddison? I am trying to help you and get the care that you need if you are really pregnant." He stood over here as she was locked in like an insane person in the straight jacket. Her eyes were ill-fated as the man she hated walked in. "Maddison, I am here trying to help you. Please listen to me very carefully...I will say this once and only once. If you test positive for your baby, I will make sure that you get to hold your baby when it's born. Also, that Brody is here to witness it also." Agent Stone had a soft spot for mother's-to-be and would make sure she had rights, even though he did not like the little bitch that spit in his face like he was a nobody. He was one of the top men in the FBI and would not take orders from crazy people. He reached for his stomach to let her know he did believe her about there being a baby in her womb. "Maddison, I want to let you know that the baby will be put in the best of care later and I give you my word on that." Her eyes felt the sting of the burn from the dry eyes as her soul would be tore apart in this web of losing her child. It was not his fucking say how a mother raises her child, "No, the baby stays with me and the father. Don't you understand that?!" She was mad and would put him away soon, the killing would bring peace at last. The sounds of her man's voice came into her head as if they were her inner thoughts for they were one. 'You must kill him Maddison and we will have this child together'. She could see his face as clear as the brightest star shining down on the earth from above. He sat there in his cell. The control was endless as he owned her. After sex had happen and his baby was in her now, he was her master and she was at his mercy. It had entered her like a virus building and killing the good cells, making her die inside little by little until she was evil to the core.

She fell back as her body was off of the table like a magic trick in front of the big crowd.

Agent Stone looked in horror as the woman had been breaking the belts on the table like they were strings, one by one they popped off like fireworks. He could not take his eyes off of her as she stared into him with the burning eyes of fire then they changed to burning red flames. "You can't do shit and you dare take my baby?" Agent Stone went for his waist band 38 revolver, but it was like it weighed over 100 pounds of pure steel. Maddison lifted the agent above the floor and as he spun in a 360 degree pattern, his eyes closed as he screamed for help. He went higher in the air, his head was pointing down at the floor in a 90 degree angle. Her head tilted as her hand waved in a goodbye motion. His head crashed into the floor with such force that his head became like a bloody watermelon smashed to pieces.

Her body was a woman and her strength was more of a monster as she was now a partner in crime and was now his doer in the evil way. She would be his killing machine and nobody could stop them. Her mouth came to a smile as she was not human anymore and enjoyed the bloody carnage that Brody had bestowed in her mind and body. She sat there and laughed as more bodies would fall soon.

Chapter 20
The killing machines

Maddison made her way over to Brody's cell. He saw her standing there, bloodied like she had been working at the slaughter house, killing for a living. She had gone on a rampage killing everyone in her path as if it were nothing more than walking down the street.

Brody's eyes saw the bloodied nightgown that Maddison was wearing. She put her face up to the cell and placed her lips through the bars for a kiss. "Baby, I am here and mommy came for her man." Brody rushed over as he planted a big kiss on her. "You heard me talking to you? I knew you would come by, let me out. Baby we can be together." Maddison looked him in the eyes with love and passion, she knew she could not be with him but needed him by her side. Maddison looked at the key hole, she could see the inside clear and started unlocking it as if a key were inside doing the magic. The locked clicked as was now open and ready for his escape from the cell that housed Florida's number one enemy and now Florida had a number two enemy. It felt like it was a new Bonnie and Clyde roaming the 1980s as a mass murdering couple with child on the way. She kissed him as if her soul was taking on more of the evil that held his aura in the evil sense. "I missed you Mrs. Bransford." "Well, you did not ask for my hand in marriage yet, now did you, Mr. Bransford?" She was now his and he loved her and would never hurt her like the other ones, even monsters need love, too. Their eyes were now glowing red as the FBI holding facility had been glowing with blood all over the place.

They left looking at the train wreck that had been a total murdering spree. It had been Brody's intention to have a partner in crime and she was now stronger than him and could do things that no human could do. She opened the lock with her mind as it was only as easy as sticking a key inside and opening it. "Babe, I want to take you somewhere great, just you wait." She smiled as she had known he was going to knock her off her feet as a man. He looked down at one of the guards that had her tongue cut out and eyes her were gone as the monster had a part of her mind. He saw the woman wiggling as she was trying to catch her breath. Maddison picked up her foot with one motion, she came down full force and crushed the head with one stomp as the gore was leaking out like jelly. "So much for that dumb bitch." She smiled, but it was not her smiling but the evil spirt that had her by his fingers as she was his killing machine. He had seen the many bodies that had piled up. He smiled and knew she was the one for him.

The reign of terror

Maddison's car has been there and it was great that she busted me out. I knew she had heard me to kill and she had worked her magic like a show stopper of a sort. The body count was over 30 or 35 bodies that lay on the bloodied floors that became a murder house. I was driving her black Trans Am, it was a car after my own heart. I had the blue one and now we shared the Trans Am. She had been sleeping in the passenger seat like a baby. Her outfit was changed into a cops uniform, the light blue with the dark blue hat and we matched like twins going out.

I was on my way to the House of Diamonds.

The radio came on and the reports were as follows, "Good afternoon ladies and gentlemen, we have a breaking announcement for your up to the minute news stories. Reports are coming in as a mass killing happened at the Gainesville FBI headquarters. More than 50 prison staff and several of the prisoners have escaped and are roaming the local streets, killing random people. If you hear this, please make your way home now."

He knew they would be out looking for them and needed to get away from this detention facility fast. She grabbed his hand as they made it out through the front door. It was like a mass murdering couple had taken out all of the FBI. "We are going to have so much fun now and I can't handle waiting for the baby," he said to Maddison. He gave her a look as his demons were coming out to party in the town.

The smell was iron from all of the blood loss that had gone on.

Maddison looked down at one of the officers that had been ripped apart. His eyes were gone. Maddison had been the one to give him a new appearance for the newspapers. She reached down in his eye socket and scooped some of the remaining blood to write a message for the authorities to come. Her finger went into a beautiful writing position and she wrote the words in blood that spelled out, "The found religion has been awakened".

They looked at each other and she feed some of the blood to Brody to get a taste for their work. He thought it had tasted like stale red wine that was fermented.

The door was blue with a push handle to open, and as they were coming out, two cops pulled up in a Crown Victoria. They exited the doors with a thunderous dash, two 38 Specials came out of the holsters in a cowboy-like fashion. "Get down on the ground and put your hands above your head!" The mustached cop yelled with authority to the 'new found religion of killing anyone that got in their way'.

The two lovers with blood tattered on their clothing had looked like they were eating people and drinking their blood like they had a glass of red wine for supper. The couples eyes flowed red like crimson fire raged and kept them looking insane. "Well, if it isn't Tweedle Dee and Tweedle Dum!" Brody let out a condescending remark to the two cops. They knew that more cops would be coming within minutes if they did not take care of business soon. Maddison was now the stronger one of the two as the evil spirit was pushing it through her veins like an ivy giving nutrients for the body. She looked up and as the sky was now turning black, it was going to rain severely at any second.

Maddison twirled her finger in a circle, the two cop's guns were turning towards their heads. The voices were in shock as nothing came out. It felt like it was a silent movie back in the 20s, then the two guns went off in unison. The bullets hit the two cops with such force that it looked like a 50 caliber sniper rifle had been sent off point blank, the holes that had been left in the supernatural event had left its mark on the targets. "My hands can do anything, and I mean anything," she had whispered in his ear as she kissed him in loving respect for the way she was now. The darkness had been the right fit for the new glory that had arisen. This cop car will make a nice explosion for the police to find their way faster.

Some of the bystanders were running and taking cover behind some the cars parked on the street in the two lane street.

Maddison thought in her mind that it was clear and ready to ignite this marvelous explosion of the black and white cruiser that had been the poor soul's that had got in the couple's way. Brody was growing weaker as the holy hell had been transferred to the new person and it would make the next one much greater versus the former demon possession of the monster. The flames started from the gas tank as if a match had been struck and dumped inside in one quick motion. The couple smiled as if they were watching a beautiful sunset.

Maddison's body went into a trance as her mind was in a dark place that only she could get away from, but had to fight before it was too late to get back. She was in purgatory as it was neither hell or heaven. Her father had come into the black abyss with his voice and had been real as fuck. "Daddy!" She screamed at the top of her lungs. But it was no use, her vision was there but she was not. "Daddy!" She cried for him, he was in at the bar and the man killed him right in front of her and tore out his throat. She closed her eyes and he came to her as if he were an angel flying over her head like a hawk gliding through the sky. He was not in his form, but a voice and she could feel his energy and the smell was his, for sure. "Maddison, you have to go back, your time is not up yet. You must destroy the evil within." "Daddy, I cant get back, I need your help, please!" She tried to grab him but the air just went through her hands like it was not real. "You must destroy the evil and now."

It was gone like it had been a dream, her heart racing and pounding in her chest. She had seen the monster leave her body like a whiplash had knocked her over. Her mind was right and she was now back to herself. Why was she doing this and how many people had she killed. She had seen him and it was not Brody that stood before like some stranger. The heat came off like something of pure fire and it seemed that it was not the car that had caught on fire. The people were running as the vehicle had been on fire and was about to burst at the seams. Maddison spotted a hammer and had only one chance to save her and the baby before he killed both of them. It hung on his belt loop. The small ball pein hammer had dried blood that stuck to the hammer. Maddison grabbed it as fast as she could, Brody caught her hand as if someone was trying to pick pocket and got caught. Brody grabbed her by her throat and lifted her off the ground with ease. "Ahhhh!" The sound as that was the only sound. Maddison's remembered her childhood, as the darkness came upon her deeper and deeper. Six shots fired from a revolver sounding gun. The noise from the gun shots brought her back to reality. Blood had been sprayed all over her with an amount of super soaker status. His grip let go as he laid down on the ground with holes going through his body. Maddison looked up as she saw her captain standing there, holding a smoking cop-issued gun that he had kept for safe keeping. "McDonald, how did you know I was here?" She looked up with tears running down her face. "I was called by Agent Stone and he told me you were here, so I rushed over."

Brody tried to get up as he was falling, He said, "I love you Maddison, You belong to me!" Captain McDonald reloaded one bullet and pulled the trigger, the last bullet piercing his head and came out the back with such force that the brain matter looked like a nuclear explosion. As his body was dead, the evil entity had left Brody for good.

Her body flew back and the force was beyond anything she had felt. The last thing she felt was a burning sensation in her stomach. She passed out from the pain.

Chapter 21
Florida State Prison

The time had flown by like some form of time fast forwarding. It had been one year since the massacre that Maddison Stranz had lived through and died almost by the hands of Brody Bransford.

It had been hard being a cop and now a convict serving time while awaiting sentencing for the killings at the FBI headquarters in Gainesville. The good thing is that her old captain had come to her rescue before Brody had strangled her.

I wish I had my baby, it's hell without him, tears rolled down her face like a river raging war on the boats that traveled down it. Maddison knew that her baby, Maria Stranz, was in a good home away from evil. But, her heart had felt like it was squeezed like a ripe tomato.

"Maddison your sentencing is today and you can't miss it." The guard said with a friendly canter towards her. Alex Rivera had been her guard since that frightful day, 365 days ago. He was the only thing that got her through it. She had recalled his voice telling her, that her baby would be in good hands. Her beautiful blond hair and stunning green eyes had been like her father. She hated looking at her sometimes as it was a quick reminder of the horror that lead up to this. Her birthday was coming up soon and the foster parents would be coming by for a visit. But first the sentence and she thought about it long and hard. She had played the crazed possessed person that was driven to kill the innocent at will. The count had been somewhere near 30 FBI workers. They had called it the "Devil's Possession" and it was big headlines and one of, if not, the worst massacres in the record books today.

He came back with the cuffs and in his tidy uniform. He had been rather sexy as if he was Patrick Swayze from the movies. He would have been the perfect man, she thought, vividly. "Sorry I have to do this, it's no choice for me. Please don't hold it against me, Miss Stranz." He had put his hand over his heart as if he was giving thanks to the American flag. "Alex, you can call me Maddison. We are on a different level now and we can just enjoy each other's company." She blew him a kiss with love. His cheeks were blushing as he had a crush on this woman, but he had worried that she would get him sent to prison. Her body had hurt her and now the cravings were less and less to kill some random person. Brody had infected her and passed this gawd awful spirit to her through intercourse.

It had been quiet and the time was now if he was going have sex with Maddison before she left on the bus for her sentence. Alex had not believed that she was this evil killer that the papers had made her out to be.

"Maddison? If I wanted to be with you, would you give a guy like me a chance?" Her mouth quivered as her words came with her emotion. "You are the type of man that my father would be proud for his daughter to date."

He walked as he checked either way for someone to barge in on them and send his ass to jail. His mind was set now and he needed some of that sweet pie that she had to offer. He came face to face with her and as her hand went to his member with a passionate touch, it made her excited to touch a man. Her eyes blurred by the blindness that had taken her life and turned it into her own. The feel of the dark came over her as if it had slept dormant in her inner soul. Her bones twisted and pulled as the shape had changed and grew from her petite size, she fell to the ground with a thunderous plow to the concrete floor. Her eyes opened and the glow of crimson blood had been her eye color. Alex rushed to her side as he had noticed that the woman that he had known to love and care for the last year of his life, the last thing he would ever think of next was his life would be taken for the thrill of the monster's sick mind. As it had devoured Brody's with such force and transcended him to another person by the way of the Ouija board that gave the most sinister human to ever live during his reign of terror. Now the hunt was for revenge as he had been executed in this very same prison many decades ago.

Alex rolled her over and the most terrorizing scene his eyes would ever see again.

"Hey, Alex...oh my God!" His face was missing the eyes that once had been there and the prisoner was gone.

The End

"82" Year of the Monster

By Brandon Burnside

Edited by Paul LeBlond

Made in the USA
Columbia, SC
08 November 2022